orca sports

OFF THE RIM

SONYA SPREEN BATES

ORCA BOOK PUBLISHERS

Library and Archives Canada Cataloguing in Publication

Bates, Sonya Spreen, author
Off the rim / Sonya Spreen Bates.
(Orca sports)

Issued in print and electronic formats.
ISBN 978-1-4598-0888-1 (pbk.). —ISBN 978-1-4598-0889-8 (pdf).—
ISBN 978-1-4598-0890-4 (epub)

I. Title. II. Series: Orca sports
PS8603.A8486O34 2015   jC813'.6   C2014-906679-1
                                        C2014-906680-5

First published in the United States, 2015
Library of Congress Control Number: 2014952063

Summary: Dylan struggles to focus on basketball playoffs when his girlfriend,
Jenna, becomes the target of threats from an anonymous cyberbully.

FSC

MIX
Paper from
responsible sources
FSC® C016245
www.fsc.org

*Orca Book Publishers is dedicated to preserving the environment and has printed
this book on Forest Stewardship Council® certified paper.*

Orca Book Publishers gratefully acknowledges the support for its publishing
programs provided by the following agencies: the Government of Canada through
the Canada Book Fund and the Canada Council for the Arts, and the Province of
British Columbia through the BC Arts Council and
the Book Publishing Tax Credit.

Cover photography by Corbis Images
Author photo by Megan Bates

ORCA BOOK PUBLISHERS
PO Box 5626, Stn. B
Victoria, BC Canada
V8R 6S4

ORCA BOOK PUBLISHERS
PO Box 468
Custer, WA USA
98240-0468

www.orcabook.com
Printed and bound in Canada.

18 17 16 15 • 4 3 2 1

For Russell

Chapter One

"It's no good," said Stretch, wincing as Coach Scott moved his knee back and forth. "The doc said if I did the ligament again, I'd have to have surgery. I'm out for the season."

I tried to look sympathetic, but my heart was jumping. I'd spent three years being backup to Stretch Morrison and now was my chance. Not that I'm a bad center or anything. In fact, I'm pretty damn good, if I do say so myself. But when the coach had the choice between a six-foot-seven giant (that's Stretch) and a six-foot-three all-rounder (that's me, Dylan Lane), the giant won every time. I didn't blame Coach. Stretch was good. Really good. He was hoping to go to UCLA on a basketball scholarship next year. If his knee held out.

It was halftime in the last game before the playoffs. Our team, the Mountview Hunters, versus the Fort Vancouver Trappers, and it was sudden death. Only one of us would move into the playoffs. It was game over for the losers.

Coach Scott gave Stretch's knee one last prod, then shook his head.

"Lane, you're in," he said.

Yes!

"All right, men, listen up," he continued. "I want man-to-man defense, a full-court press. It's been close so far, but we can't let them get a run on us. Dylan, control the defense boards. Box out and rebound, then follow up with a quick outlet. We want a fast turnaround. Matt, watch number 10. If you let him open up, he'll score. The rest of you know what to do. Keep the pressure up. Let's win this thing."

The whistle blew and we ran onto the court. A few kids in the stands clapped and yelled, "Go, Hunters! Carve 'em up!" There wasn't a huge crowd, but a bunch of rowdy teenagers can make a lot of noise, and so far the home-court advantage was working in our favor. We'd kept our lead for most of the game, with the halftime score 68–64 for us.

The Trappers center was tall but slow. I'd been watching him, and it looked like he was carrying a bit of weight. I, on the other hand, was in the best shape of my basketball career. I was pretty sure I could beat him to the rebounds.

It was our possession. Isaiah passed the ball in to Carlos, and he brought the ball up the court. The Trappers manned up as soon as he crossed the half-court line. I dodged around the Trappers center and charged into the key as Carlos wove through the defense. He dribbled left, then right, pivoted and fired the ball to Matt.

Matt passed it off to me, and I passed it to Isaiah, our shooting guard. We'd practiced this drill so many times we could do it in our sleep. Isaiah went in for the layup. Two points.

The crowd cheered and stamped their feet.

We had a six-point lead now. But it wasn't time to celebrate. The Trappers point guard brought the ball up the court, and I stuck to their center like glue. He wasn't going to get a touch if I could help it.

The point guard was coming up the court slowly, trying to find the open man and trying to shake his defender at the same time. Carlos was all over him, and he couldn't get a pass away. He put the ball between his legs, spun, then faked a pass to their small forward. Carlos lunged, and suddenly the Trappers guard was off. He raced over the half-court line and fired a pass at number 10, their power forward, who went up for the jump shot. Swish. A three-pointer.

I glared at Matt. So much for shutting down number 10.

On offense again, Carlos managed to get a quick pass off to Spence. I tried to ditch the Trappers center and open up for the ball, but he was quicker than I'd thought. Every way I turned, he was there. Spence threw the ball off to Matt instead, and Matt bounce-passed it to Isaiah. Isaiah drove for the basket but was brought up short by a defensive wall in front of the basket. He turned and passed it back to Matt.

That's when number 10 swooped in and intercepted. Before we knew what had happened, he was racing down the court for a fast break layup.

Our six-point lead was down to one.

Spence scored the next two points with an easy jump shot, and then number 10 found the basket for another two. Unbelievable.

Matt looked miserable as Coach Scott called for a sub. I felt for the guy. No one wants to get benched for messing up. But we had to do something to shut down number 10. I only hoped Jesse Derby was up to the job. He wasn't nearly as big as Matt, more like a small forward than a power forward. But he was quick, and he didn't mind playing dirty if he had to.

The shot clock turned over, and Carlos went up for a three. We needed every point we could get. It bounced off the rim. I snatched the rebound, faked a pass to Isaiah, then popped it in for two. The quarter raced on. We'd get ahead two, maybe four points, and then the Trappers would catch up. Even with Jesse right in his face, number 10 still managed to weasel out for an assist. With only three minutes left on the clock, it was down to the wire, and neither team was giving an inch.

The Trappers coach called a time-out, and we crowded onto the bench.

"All right, settle down," Coach said as we grabbed our water bottles. "It's close, but we're still a point up, and a point is a win. We've got to tighten the defense. Don't let them near that basket. Jesse, keep the pressure on number 10. And Carlos, watch your check. He's gone for a couple of threes, and if he sinks one, we're done. Isaiah, you're our go-to guy. Keep those buckets coming."

We huddled in a circle and stacked our hands on top of Coach Scott's, then let fly with, "HUNTERS!"

My stomach was wound as tight as a rubber band as I took my position on the court. It was all or nothing. With graduation only months away, this was my last chance to be a starter in the playoffs. There wouldn't be a next year for me. I glanced at the stands, where Jenna was camped with the rest of the girls' basketball team in the front row. I cracked a smile at her, and she yelled, "Go, Dylan!"

"Yeah, go, Dylan!" Amber Wells called out, jumping out of her seat. "Go, Hunters!" Jenna hauled her back into her seat, laughing. Easy for them to laugh. They'd been on the top of the ladder all season. There was no doubt about their playoff spot.

The whistle blew and the Trappers streamed onto the court. It was game on.

Carlos dribbled the ball over the half-court line and lobbed an easy pass to Spence. The Trappers had set up a zone defense, protecting the key. I dodged past their guard into the paint and spun for the pass, only to find the Trappers center right behind me. Spence passed to Isaiah, who faked a pass to Jesse. We all knew better than to let the ball near number 10. The fake did the trick though. The defender reached for the steal, and Isaiah charged in for the layup. I could see right away he'd never make it. The Trappers center had set a block, and there was no getting around that six-foot-six hulk to the basket. I ducked around the other side and called for the ball.

The ref's whistle blew. "Three seconds on 43, Mountview! Blue ball."

No! I spun around in disbelief, but the ref was already handing the ball over to the Trappers guard. Had I really done that? That turnover could mean the difference between winning and losing. Had I lost the game for the whole team on a stupid lane violation?

There was no time to dwell on it. The Trappers had possession, and I raced down the court after the center. My screw-up must have given him wings because before I'd crossed the three-point line, he was in the key. The point guard fired a long pass to him, and he dunked it.

I felt sick. The Trappers were up, and it was my fault.

I jogged back down the court and camped myself on the block. I wasn't going to let that happen again. I couldn't let that happen again, or we were done.

Carlos brought the ball down, shadowed by his defender, despite the zone they'd set up around the key. They weren't taking any chances either. He spun around, faked a pass to Spence and then fired it to Isaiah. I dipped into the key, boxing out the Trappers center for the rebound. I needn't have bothered. Isaiah went up for a killer jump shot and hit the three.

Yes!

The minutes raced by at the speed of light. The Trappers scored another two, and then Carlos nailed a jump shot from the wing. The kids in the stands were screaming. If we couldn't shut the Trappers down completely, we made them work for their baskets. We were two points up, with twenty seconds left on the clock, when Jesse fouled number 10.

Number 10! Of all the players, we had to give number 10 two free shots. This could even up the score.

He had to be feeling the pressure. He wiped his hands down his shirt, looked up and let the ball fly, sinking the first shot with a swish. You could see his relief. His teammates thumped him on the back, and the ball was passed back for the second shot. He bounced it once, twice, three times. I leaned in, ready for the rebound. I saw the ball arcing toward the rim. The rim! I couldn't believe it. He'd missed.

I bounded into the key and leapt for the rebound. The Trappers center was there too. We tussled. I ripped the ball away and fired a pass to Carlos on the three-point line. Everyone was focused on the rebound.

He was wide open. Carlos raced down the court like a demon, with all the Trappers and Hunters trailing behind him. He dribbled the full length of the court and dunked the ball on the other end.

It was all over after that. The Trappers had one more possession, but we didn't let them anywhere near the basket. The final buzzer sounded, and the gym exploded. We'd done it. We were in the playoffs.

Chapter Two

The next day, Coach Scott posted the list for the playoff team. Jenna saw it first. In the year we'd been going out, I hadn't learned to tell whether she was being serious or not. She sidled up to me at my locker and slid her hand into mine.

"Hey, Dyl, I saw the list," she said, totally deadpan.

"For the playoffs? Coach posted them?"

"Yeah, I thought you would have seen it already."

"No, I had to see Mr. Chandler about a math test I missed." Damn it. The whole school probably knew already whether I was a starter or coming off the bench. I slammed my locker shut and headed for the gym.

"Am I one of the starters? Did you see the lineup?"

Jenna just shrugged and gave me a look. One that could mean everything or nothing.

I had to start center. I knew I had screwed up, but who else could Coach put in? Matt? He was our best power forward. We needed him there. There was Noah too, but he was hopeless. He didn't even get subbed in if it was an important game. It couldn't be Noah, could it? No, Coach wouldn't do that to me. He wouldn't do that to the team, would he?

The notice board outside the gym was crowded with lists. Mountview High might be a small-town school, but we liked our sports. We had a team for everything, from football, soccer and baseball to wrestling, bowling and cheerleading.

The basketball list was at the top of the board. I scanned it quickly. Coach had a funny way of doing things. You would have thought Carlos Abano would be at the top of the list, *A* being the first letter of the alphabet. Nope. Coach did things his own way. Even posting a starter list before the playoffs was pretty out there. I read from the top of the list: Spencer Zuckerman. Then Matt Garth, Isaiah Noble, Carlos Abano and...Dylan Lane. Yes!

I guess I looked pretty relieved, because Jenna burst out laughing.

"You knew!" I said. "You knew and you didn't tell me."

"I didn't want to spoil it for you," she said. "Not that there was any doubt. Jeez, Dylan, who did you think he'd put in? Noah Walker?" She started laughing again. I couldn't hide anything from her. "You did. You actually thought Coach Scott would pick Noah Stumblefoot over you. He wants to win the playoffs, Dyl, not throw them away."

That reminded me though. With Stretch out, we were short one sub. Coach might not have a choice about playing Noah.

He and Jesse Derby were the only subs left. Our playoff run could be pretty short.

The bell rang for class, and Jenna said she had to go. She has this thing about being late. "Hey," I said, catching her arm. "There's no practice after school. Want a ride home tonight?"

"Yes!" she said. "Like I'd choose to sit on the school bus for an hour if I didn't have to." She winked at me. "See you at three."

Jenna's got this dual personality. She can be all social and flirty, but there's a serious side to her too. It's one of the things I like about her. She's got these funny little quirks. Take being late, for instance. It drives her insane. And leaving a mess on the table at a fast-food joint. She has to put everyone's trash in the can before we leave. She won't eat anything with lumps in it, and if I go even five miles an hour over the speed limit, she goes berserk. She's also really smart and the best female point guard I've seen. Ever. We play one-on-one at the rec center sometimes and she gives me a run for my money, even though I'm five inches taller than she is. She could sink a basket from the parking lot.

She was leaning on my car as I crossed the student lot after school. I checked my watch.

"You're early," I said.

"You're late," she countered. Was she serious or not?

"I'm not. I left as soon as the bell—" I caught the look in her eye and realized I'd been duped again. "Ha-ha," I said. "Get in."

"You sure this thing will make it all the way to Eaton Creek?" she said as I started up the engine. It was an ongoing joke. My rusty 2004 Honda Civic wasn't the best-looking or the most powerful car in the student lot, but I'd spent two summers working my butt off at McDonald's to pay for it. It was my pride and joy.

"You sure you don't want to walk?" I said.

As usual, we stopped at Jo's Diner for a soda before we left town. It was a favorite after-school hangout for most of the Mountview students, and even on a Tuesday afternoon, it was crowded. I spied Carlos, Spence and Matt at a booth in the back, and we squeezed in with them.

"What can I get for you?" said Jo, standing over us with her pen and order pad at the ready. Jo's cool. Every afternoon all these kids take over her place and spend, like, five bucks, but she still acts like you're going to order a five-course meal or something.

I was feeling like a splurge. "A chocolate shake and a plate of fries," I said.

"Diet Coke," said Jenna. "Celebrating, are you?" she said when Jo left.

"No," I said with a glance at the guys. "I'm just hungry."

The talk was all about the first round of the playoffs. With the game scheduled for next week, we didn't have much time to prepare.

"Columbia's a hard draw," said Carlos, slumped over the table as if he'd heard he had some incurable disease or something. You'd think we'd drawn the San Antonio

Spurs the way he was acting. "They went all the way to the state finals last year. We'll get creamed in the first round."

"That doesn't mean anything," said Matt. "Different team, different guys. It's a whole new ball game." Carlos scowled at him, and Matt leaned back into the booth. "Look at us. Last year's team didn't have a hope of making it to the playoffs, and here we are."

"Don't get too cocky," said Spence. "It could have gone either way with the Trappers. We lucked out."

"Yeah," said Carlos. "And we've lost our big man. What are we gonna do without Stretch?"

"Thanks for the vote of confidence," I said as Jo put my milkshake and fries in front of me.

"No offense, Dylan," said Carlos, stealing a couple of fries off my plate, "but let's face it. You're good, but you're not Stretch."

I couldn't argue with that. I took a couple of fries and pushed the plate to the middle of the table. There's no point trying to keep a plate of fries to yourself when you're with a group of hungry teenagers.

"And we're going to have to play Noah Walker," said Spence as he grabbed a handful for himself.

Carlos put his head in his hands. "I don't even want to think about that," he moaned.

"He's not that bad," said Matt.

We all glared at him. "Yes he is," we chorused.

Matt grinned sheepishly. "Yeah, I guess he is. Maybe if he practiced a bit..."

"The problem with Noah," said Jenna, "is his confidence. He thinks he's crap, so he plays like crap."

"He *is* crap," said Carlos.

"But if he had more confidence in himself, he would play better," said Jenna.

"What are you, the new sports psychologist?" said Carlos.

Jenna shrugged. "Fine. If you don't want my help..."

"What are you going to do?" said Spence. "Teach him to play basketball in ten easy lessons? He's been playing since freshman year. We've only got a week until the first playoff game."

"Eight days, to be exact," said Carlos. "But who's counting?"

I could see Jenna wasn't going to let this go. She could be stubborn when she wanted to. She pointed her finger at Carlos. "I bet you I can teach Noah Walker to play better before the next game."

"Yeah?" said Carlos, eyeing her curiously. "What's on the line?"

Jenna looked around the restaurant. "The loser buys everyone a round of sodas after the game," she said.

"You're on," said Carlos.

"How are we going to tell if he's playing better?" asked Matt. "That's pretty vague."

There was a pause, and then Carlos folded his arms across his chest. "He has to sink one," he said. He gestured toward Jenna. "If you can get Noah to sink a basket in the first round, I will gladly buy the whole team a round of sodas. Including Noah Walker."

"It's a deal," said Jenna.

"We have so much work to do," said Jenna as I started the car.

"We?" I said. "What's this *we*? You're the one who made the bet. Don't drag me into it." I pulled out onto Railroad Avenue and headed north.

"Come on, Dylan," said Jenna. "You know I can't do this without you. Besides, don't you want Noah to improve his game? You guys keep saying he's crap, but you don't want to do anything about it. Do you want to win the playoffs or not?"

She had a point. Of course we wanted to win the playoffs. Or at least make it through to the regional semis. Noah was our weak man, and any help we could give him would only benefit the team. Hell, if he started playing better, we might actually have a chance. The problem would be talking Noah into extra practices. He was the biggest nerd in the school. Basketball came a distant third or fourth to debating, Mathletics and the annual science competition.

"Yeah, all right," I said. "I'll help him train, but it's up to you to pry him off his computer."

She sat back, satisfied.

I turned off the highway onto Hillridge Road. It felt almost like turning onto my own street, I'd driven it so many times in the last year. It was starting to get dark, so I flicked on my lights. Jenna put the radio on, and a Bruno Mars song drifted into the car. Bruno Mars wasn't really my thing, but I knew Jenna loved him, so I cranked it up and we sped up the hill belting out "Marry You." It's one of those songs that gets stuck in your head after hearing it, but we didn't care.

As we approached Devil's Bend, I slowed down. On this side of the mountain, there wasn't much sun in winter, and old crusty snow still lay at the side of the road. I navigated the corner carefully, aware of the fifty-foot drop on the other side of the protective barrier. Just as I started to speed up out of the turn, headlights loomed behind me. The glare shone directly into my rearview mirror, blinding me on one side.

Jenna turned off the radio and glanced out the rear window. "Where did he come from?"

"I don't know," I said, trying to drive with one hand while shielding my eyes from the glare with the other. "But I wish he'd back off. I can't see a thing."

The driver of the vehicle honked his horn. Not a friendly little toot but a drawn-out, ear-splitting blast that set my heart racing. As if it wasn't already.

"What does he want me to do? It's not like I can pull over," I said. I gripped the steering wheel tightly, navigating the next corner with difficulty. I didn't want to slow down, but I didn't have much choice.

The vehicle surged closer. I half expected to feel a slam on my bumper. The driver blasted his horn again. Over and over.

"What is he doing?" cried Jenna.

My palms started to sweat, which did nothing for my control of the car. We rounded the next corner and headed into a straight patch of road.

"All right," I said. "You're in such a hurry. Pass me already."

The vehicle pulled out into the next lane, and I slowed down to let him by. I'd be glad to see the back of him, whoever he was. Expecting him to roar past, I was surprised when he crept up alongside me.

"Come on," I shouted. "The passing lane's not that long. Get going!"

I glanced over at the vehicle. It was a brand-new black F-150 pickup. I couldn't see the driver through the darkened window. Suddenly the truck swerved toward me. I yanked the steering wheel hard to the right and felt the crunch of gravel under the tires.

I swore. Loudly. I couldn't help it. The car bumped along the shoulder as I tried to ease it back onto the pavement. The next bend in the road was coming up quickly.

The truck driver blasted his horn and swerved toward us again. Jenna screamed.

It was then that I saw the oncoming headlights. Rounding the bend and approaching fast. The pickup swung into my lane. I hit the brakes, but not quickly enough. The rear bumper of the truck clipped the front of the car, and we went into a spin. My headlights flashed on pine trees and bushes, and my ears rang with the sound of screams and horns. I don't remember slamming into the tree.

Chapter Three

The cop who showed up at the scene was the same one who came to our school every year to give lectures on safe driving. She had a thing about kids and accidents. I tried to explain about the black pickup, and Jenna backed me up, but the lady in the other car told wild stories of two cars drag-racing down the road, almost killing her. She was hysterical. Not that I was in very good shape. I must have blacked out for a second because I didn't remember hitting the tree and I was shaking like the proverbial leaf.

Jenna was great about the whole thing. I'm embarrassed to admit that she kept it together way better than I did. She talked to the cop first while I sat by the side of the road, wrapped in an emergency blanket, staring at what was left of my car. You hear horror stories about car accidents, and we all slow down to have a look at a crash on the side of the road, but you never really believe it will happen to you until it does.

The cops had a search on for the black pickup. They said if they found the right vehicle, they'd be able to prove it was involved in the accident. And the driver's testimony would either back up my story or the hysterical lady's. The problem was, the truck seemed to have vanished off the face of the earth. No one had seen it tailing us up Hillridge Road. No one remembered seeing it in town. No one knew anyone who owned a truck like that. Gone. And I was left to take the blame. I got a ticket for "driving too fast for the conditions" and

Jenna's parents forbade her from ever getting in a car with me again. Not to mention that my car was towed to the garage, and I was without wheels for the foreseeable future. Things couldn't get much worse.

My dad pulled the parent card and made me stay home the next day. I hated to miss practice, but at the same time my head felt about the size of a basketball, and I was happy to sleep in. When I arrived at school on Thursday morning for before-school practice, all the guys had already heard about the accident. I think Jenna posted something on Facebook about the black pickup. Not a bad strategy, really. If you want to reach a lot of people fast, Facebook is the way to go.

"Hey," said Carlos, giving me a slap on the back. "Bummer about your car. Can they fix it?"

"Yeah. I've got it at the body shop. It's going to cost me though." More than I could afford, really. Together, the repairs and the ticket cost almost as much as the car itself. Another reason I needed to find the driver of that black pickup. If I could prove that he was the one driving recklessly, he'd have to pay to fix up my car, and I'd be off the hook.

"Are you going to play today?"

"Of course I am," I said. "Why wouldn't I?"

"Because of that goose egg on the side of your head?" Carlos said, pointing to the bump above my left ear. I must have hit it on the side window, though I couldn't remember.

"That?" I shrugged. "It's not as bad as it looks. Let's go."

The gym was freezing at this time of the morning. Coach Scott ran us through the usual warm-up and then set up some drills. He'd taught us a new offensive play this year. It worked like a dream. When everyone knew what to do, that is. Bring in Jesse Derby and Noah Walker, and everything fell apart. They had missed too many practices to get it.

In fact, Jesse Derby hadn't even bothered to show up this morning. Yeah, it was early, yeah, it was cold, but this was the playoffs. You couldn't just rock up and expect to win. Noah Walker was at least trying.

Coach ran through a pass-to-the-corner drill, then two kinds of dribble-drive drills. I could see Noah was trying to figure out how they went together. For a smart guy, he was pretty dumb about basketball plays. He couldn't figure out when to stay in the corner and when to rotate up to take the pass. My head was throbbing, and it was getting pretty frustrating. For all of us. Finally, Coach blew the whistle, and we all headed for the showers. Except Noah. Coach pulled him aside, a hand on his arm. I didn't know what he said, but Noah looked absolutely miserable when he followed us in a few minutes later.

The mood in the locker room was pretty low. For once Matt wasn't cracking jokes, and Carlos and Spence weren't horsing around. Noah got changed quickly and gathered up his stuff. I think we all thought our playoff dreams were over. I hadn't thought about Jenna's bet since the accident, but it came back now, having seen Noah's performance that morning. I knew Jenna, and when she put her mind to something, she did it. Could she really help Noah improve his game? It was worth a shot.

"Noah, wait up," I said as he headed out into the corridor. He looked surprised. Although we'd played basketball together for four years, we rarely talked to each other off the court. "I was thinking," I said. "We all want to do well against Columbia next week, right?"

He shrugged. "Yeah. Of course we do."

"Well, you know," I said. "Coach isn't always the best at showing how things work. Like game plays and such. I thought maybe you'd like to go through a few plays together."

He stopped and looked at me. "You think I'm hopeless, don't you?"

"No! You're not hopeless," I lied. "It's just...you know, it's playoffs and...Stretch is injured and I thought a little extra practice..."

"Yeah, I get it," said Noah. He stared off into the distance, and I was sure he was going to say no. I should have let Jenna ask him.

She was way better at talking people into things than I was. "All right," he said finally.

"Yeah?"

"Yeah. What the hell," he said. "It can't hurt."

My thoughts exactly.

Chapter Four

Jesse Derby showed up at math class with a black eye. I wasn't entirely surprised. Jesse's known for being a bit of a thug. In middle school he was always the one getting sent to the principal's office for fighting in the schoolyard. When he started playing hoops, I thought he'd cleaned up his act. I guess I was wrong.

"Where were you this morning?" I said, dropping into the seat next to him.

"Hello!" said Jesse sarcastically. "See this shiner?"

"Yeah, what about it?" I said. "See this bump? It didn't stop me from going to practice."

"Well, I'm not a nutcase like you, am I?" he said, turning away.

I grabbed his arm. "Come on, Jesse, this is the playoffs," I said. "We need everyone on board."

He wrenched his arm out of my grasp. "Tell someone who cares," he said. "I've got bigger things to worry about than missing one lousy practice." He picked up his stuff and moved to a desk on the other side of the room.

I didn't get it. My philosophy was that you try out for a team, you're part of the team, and when the team needs you, you're there. If Jesse really didn't care whether we won or lost, why try out for the team at all? He was more of a mystery to me than girls.

We had scheduled a practice session with Noah at the rec center that afternoon. I wasn't 100 percent sure he would turn up. Noah didn't have the greatest track record for making it to basketball practice. Just about everything else took priority with him. As it turned out, he was there before we were. But then, he had wheels, and Jenna and I had to walk.

"What's she doing here?" he asked when he saw Jenna. I guess I'd forgotten to mention that the extra practices were her idea.

"We need a third person to demonstrate the moves," I said casually. I tried not to look at Jenna's fuming face. I guess I'd forgotten to mention to her that I'd forgotten to mention her to Noah.

Noah didn't look too happy. "I don't need it getting around school that I'm being coached by a girl," he said.

Jenna's face was getting darker by the minute. This wasn't going the way I'd hoped.

"Now hang on a minute," I said. "Jenna isn't just any girl. She's the best point guard in the school after Carlos. And that includes me and the rest of the guys on our team. I'd take pointers from her any day."

"And in case you hadn't noticed," said Jenna, "the girls' team has been winning all season. You guys just squeaked it in on the buzzer."

"Does she know the plays?" Noah was still talking to me.

"She knows the plays," I said firmly.

"And so do you," said Jenna. "You just don't know it yet."

"What's that supposed to mean?" he said.

"Have you ever heard that saying 'You can't see the forest for the trees?'" said Jenna. He nodded and she continued. "That's you. You're thinking so much about where to put your feet, and whether to dribble right or left or hold your ground, you can't see the play as a whole. You've got to forget about the small stuff and let the play do its thing."

I didn't know where she got her information, or if there was any truth to it, but it seemed to be working. Noah wasn't looking quite so skeptical anymore.

"How am I supposed to let the play 'do its thing' if I don't think about the small stuff?" he asked.

"We make a muscle memory," she said. "It's like learning to drive a car. After the first week you don't think about when to move your foot from the gas to the brake—you just do it, right? Same thing with basketball. We'll run the plays so many times you won't have to think about what to do 'cause your muscles will do the thinking for you."

Noah was nodding. "Yeah. That makes sense."

"We'll run them slowly first," she said, "until you've got the whole play, then go over it in real time."

Noah looked from me to Jenna. "All right," he said. "I'm not making any promises, but I'll give it a try." He went to find a ball in the storeroom, and I leaned in close to Jenna.

"Nice con," I said. "Did you make all that up?"

"No," she said. "I read about it online. I don't know if it'll work for basketball, but it sounded good, didn't it?" Just then her phone chirped, and she pulled it out of her pocket to check the message.

As quickly as she'd pulled the phone out, she shut it off again and shoved it into her bag. She busied herself stripping off her jacket and riffling through her books. I knew her better than that. I'd seen the look on her face.

"What?" I said. "What's wrong?"

"Nothing. What are you talking about?" she said, avoiding my gaze.

"That message. You look like you've seen a ghost."

"That? No, it wasn't anything. Nothing important. Come on, let's play ball." She ran onto the court, where Noah was practicing his layups.

We ran through the basic drills, in slow-mo first, then gradually speeding them up. Noah was clumsy. He fumbled the ball, threw his passes wild and travelled when he finished dribbling, but we just kept going. Over and over again until he started moving without thinking, anticipating the pass.

He wasn't perfect by any stretch of the imagination. But he was better, and that was all we could hope for.

We were feeling pretty good about ourselves as we finished up and agreed on a time for the next session. I think it was the first time I'd seen Noah Walker smiling and enjoying himself on the basketball court.

The next day dawned, and with it another early-morning practice. I was looking forward to the guys seeing the improvement in Noah's skills. Everyone was there. Even Jesse Derby showed up, his shiner a dull greenish color now. We'd show him the difference coming to practice made. But once Coach had run us through the warm-up, he called us in and dropped a bombshell.

"All right," he said. "This is playoffs, and we need to up our game. We're going to put in the triangle offense."

I groaned. We'd tried this play earlier in the season, and it had been a disaster. Why was Coach Scott trying to get fancy now, when we were down a man and lacking the basics in our subs? We were the Mountview Hunters, not the Chicago Bulls.

He set us up for a drill. I could see Noah's confusion straightaway. He had no idea where the ball was coming from or where he was supposed to go. Coach wasn't much help either. He just yelled at Noah, "Walker, take position! Not there. In the corner. Walker! At the top of the key! On the block, Walker!" Noah was getting more and more frustrated, as was Coach and all of us guys as well. I felt for Noah. It wasn't like the rest of us were perfect. No one knew the drill very well. But when Noah went completely the wrong way, it screwed up everyone. He was getting more than a few dirty looks.

It was almost time for the bell, and I couldn't stand it any longer. All the hard work from yesterday was being undone. I'd be lucky if Noah didn't give up altogether after this.

"Hey, Coach," I said. "Do you think we could run those drills from yesterday again?"

"Now, Lane? It's almost quitting time."

"I just want to make sure I've got it. All this new stuff is messing with my brain."

He narrowed his eyes at me but blew the whistle. "All right. Pass to the corner."

I gave Noah a nod that I hoped said, "All right. You've got this one." He didn't acknowledge it. Just took his position at the top of the key.

I've got to hand it to Jenna. Muscle memory or whatever, she'd done her job well. The first time through was a little shaky, but after that I could almost see Noah heading into the zone. Dribble in past the free-throw line. Pass to the corner. Rotate to the corner position. Take the pass and shoot. Okay, so his shots weren't going in, and his jump stop was a bit awkward. But he knew the drill. He wasn't messing anyone else up. After five minutes Coach blew the whistle and we headed for the locker room. Noah was getting a few more looks now, and so was I, but they weren't dirty looks anymore.

Chapter Five

"So he can do a pass-to-the-corner drill," said Carlos. "Big deal."

It was lunchtime, and we were huddled around a table in the cafeteria. Matt, Carlos, Jenna, Amber and me. The table was littered with the remains of salads and sandwiches, and Matt was picking the crumbs off his burger wrapper. I don't know where Matt puts all his food. He eats like a linebacker and looks like a sprinter.

"Big deal?" said Matt. "Did you see him? He hasn't played that well, like...ever. I could actually fire a normal pass at him and not worry about taking him out."

"It's one drill," said Carlos, waving his finger at us. "Wait till he's got a defender in his face and five seconds on the shot clock." Carlos was never one to look on the bright side.

"Yeah, we get that," I said. "It's not like game play. But why do you think Coach runs the drills in the first place? So we play better in the game. Give us a break. It's only been one day."

Carlos shrugged.

"You just don't want to admit we might actually win this bet," said Jenna smugly.

"I'm not sweatin' it. Catching a pass isn't the same thing as getting a shot in," said Carlos. He crumpled up his garbage and did a perfect shot into the trash can. "Nowhere near the same thing." He grabbed his stuff and headed off.

Matt slid off the bench and slung his bag over his shoulder. "Who cares what he thinks?" he said. "If you can get Noah playing, I'm all for it."

No one said anything after he left. I think we were all thinking the same thing. That what Carlos said was right. The first round was less than a week away. It was too little too late.

"So," said Amber, turning to Jenna. "Did you find out who was sending you those creepy messages?"

Jenna scowled at her in a way that clearly said, "Shut up!"

"What creepy messages?" I said. "What are you talking about?"

"It's nothing," said Jenna.

"On Facebook," said Amber.

They both spoke at the same time, and I looked back and forth from one to the other in confusion.

"Didn't you tell him?" said Amber, eyebrows raised.

Jenna glared at her. "Why would I?" she said. "It's got nothing to do with him."

"Tell me what? Jenna, what's going on?" I was starting to freak out a bit.

She wouldn't look me in the eye, and that usually meant trouble.

"Someone's been sending Jenna these creepy messages on Facebook," said Amber.

"What kind of creepy messages?" I said.

"Threats mostly."

It was a bit like the moment I knew my car was going out of control. Unreal. A these-things-don't-happen-to-people-you-know moment. "Why didn't you tell me?" I said.

"Because I knew you'd freak out, and you are," said Jenna. "Just forget about it. I can handle it."

"How?"

She looked up and glared at me. "By ignoring it. They'll get tired of it eventually and stop."

"Oh, great plan," I said. I was more than a little mad that she'd told Amber and not me. "Do nothing. Hope it goes away." Then something dawned on me. "That message you got yesterday at the rec center. It was one of them, wasn't it?" It wasn't nothing. She'd been scared. I'd seen it on her face. "How long have you been getting them?"

Jenna stared at the table and said nothing.

"A couple of weeks," said Amber. "That I know of anyway."

"A couple of weeks!" Now that I thought about it, Jenna had been a little jumpy lately. I'd been so focused on the last matches of the season that I hadn't given it any thought. "Jenna, you've got to tell someone. Who's sending them? Someone from school? We'll go to the office and tell Mr. Anderson, or the counselor, or your parents..."

"No!" She said it so loud that the kids at the next table turned to stare at us. "This is why I didn't tell you, Dylan. I'm not going to Mr. Anderson or the counselor or anyone else. If my parents found out...well, I'd never be let out of the house again. Just leave it alone."

She grabbed her books off the table and stormed out. With a shrug, Amber followed her. I was left staring at their backs and wondering what the heck I was supposed to do now.

It was obvious Jenna was still mad when we met up with Noah after school. I hadn't decided what, if anything, I was going to do about the threats. So I kept my mouth shut. She was probably right about her parents. They had always been strict and overprotective. But when Jenna had witnessed a robbery at the 7-Eleven over the Christmas holidays, their parental instincts had gone into overdrive. Ever since then, they overreacted to things big-time. Like the car accident. That black truck had hounded us. The more I'd thought about it, the more positive I was that the driver had wanted us to drive off the road. It hadn't been my fault. We'd explained what happened to Jenna's parents when the cops dropped us at her place, but you could see they were close to losing it. They kept staring at me like they'd just found out I was in a motorcycle gang or something. They claimed to believe us, but Jenna was still banned from riding with me.

We tried to act like everything was normal between us. I told Jenna about practice that morning, how Coach had sprung the new drills on us. I was hoping we could do at least one or two of them, but Jenna was set on doing some shooting drills. I think Carlos had gotten to her with the "taking a pass isn't the same as making a shot" remark.

Noah was hopeless at shooting. We ran through the drills over and over. And while he got into the groove of who to pass to and where to take the shot from, he probably scored a max of five baskets in the hour of practice.

None of us were feeling very good about it as we packed up to go.

"We should have practiced the triangle-offense drills," I said as I pulled on my jacket. If Coach ran them again next week, Noah was going to be just as lost as he had been today.

"There's no way Coach Scott is going to play the triangle offense in the playoffs," Jenna scoffed. "He's bluffing. That's way too much of a risk. Especially with the team you've got."

"What's that supposed to mean?" I said.

"Let's face it," said Jenna, rolling her eyes at Noah. "You guys aren't really championship material."

"And I suppose the girls are?" I was getting mad now. If she was looking for a fight, she was going to get it.

Her eyes flashed. She *was* looking for a fight. "My girls could beat your team any day."

"Oh yeah?" I could see Noah shaking his head, but I couldn't back down now. "Want to put your money where your mouth is?"

"Name the day," said Jenna.

"Saturday, 7:00 PM."

"You're on," said Jenna.

We stood and stared at each other. I knew this fight wasn't about whose team was better, and so did she. Neither of us was going to spell it out though. We gathered our stuff without another word.

As we followed Jenna out of the gym, Noah shook his head again. "What have you done?" he muttered.

Chapter Six

I didn't tell Coach about the game. Mountview boys versus Mountview girls. It was hard enough to sell it to the guys.

"If we lose this game, man, we'll never live it down," said Carlos.

"Yeah, and if we pull out now, they'll say we knew we couldn't win," I said. It was a lose-lose situation. Unless we won. There was no other choice.

The rec center was crowded with kids. We'd tried to keep it quiet, but word had gotten around. Boys versus girls. Everyone had come out to watch us prove which was the better sex. We had nominated Stretch as coach. Jesse Derby had better things to do on a Saturday night, or so he claimed, and that left us with one sub—Noah.

The game started out all right. We had the height advantage, so I easily beat Chelsea Collins to the tip and Carlos grabbed the ball before it even got within Amber's reach. He fired the pass to Matt, who drove in for an easy layup.

"Want to give up now?" I said to Jenna as we passed midcourt.

"We're just getting warmed up, big shot," she said.

Stretch had set us a half-court man defense. Against the girls, who were smaller than us, it was the best strategy. That didn't mean we shut them down. Bounce passes, fast breaks, three-pointers, quick dribble drive. They knew their stuff, and they were prepared to use it. They also had an eight-man—or rather eight-woman team, meaning three subs. And not a Noah Walker in sight.

By halftime we were all in. Stretch hadn't subbed anyone off, and the five of us were panting like a pack of sled dogs. We were still up though, 45–35. A comfortable lead.

"Don't start thinking we've got a comfortable lead now," said Stretch. "Ten points can disappear like that." He snapped his fingers to demonstrate. "Jenna's their biggest scorer, but she's no ball hog. She'll pass it off if she has to, so watch Chelsea and Amber as well." He looked around at us all sucking down our drinks, red-faced and sweating. "Noah, I'm going to put you on."

I don't know whose face was more comical, Noah's or the rest of the guys'. It was the last thing we'd expected.

"Come on, Stretch, you can't do that," said Carlos. "No offense, Noah, but we've got to win this thing."

"No, I've thought this through," said Stretch. "We play on Noah's strengths and avoid his weaknesses."

"His strengths?" said Carlos. "Like what?"

I could see Noah was wondering the same thing.

"Number one, his height." True. At six-foot-four, Noah even beat me in the height department. "We switch to a zone defense," continued Stretch. "Noah camps in the key, and those girls won't get anywhere near the paint for a layup. You can do that, right, Noah?"

Noah nodded. He looked interested.

"Number two, passing."

"Passing?" said Carlos. "You've got to be kidding."

"No, I was watching him yesterday," said Stretch. "His passing skills have really improved. You pass to him nice and high, over the girls' heads, and we get the ball into the paint. Noah, Spence and Isaiah are your go-to guys. You get the ball into the key and let them do the shooting. Got it?"

It made sense. And, for the first time, Noah was looking pleased about being subbed in.

"Dylan, you're off first."

We threw our hands into the middle of our circle and shouted, "Hunters!"

I was nervous watching Noah run onto the court in my place. Stretch was right—ten points could disappear really quickly. I was curious to see how he would do though. We'd had another practice that morning, running drills of every kind. Everything except the triangle-offense drills, that is. Jenna was convinced Coach Scott wouldn't run it in playoffs. Noah had improved. There was no doubt about it. He could run the drills far better than he ever had. We were about to find out if he could transfer those skills to game play.

Jenna saw him run on and nodded at me. I could tell she was just as eager as I was to prove her extra training with Noah was working.

It was the girls' ball, and Amber passed it in to Jenna to bring up the court. The guys spread out in a 2-1-2 zone, with Noah center stage in front of the hoop. It was a good spot for him. His height would stop anyone from attempting a layup if they penetrated the defense, and other than that he couldn't do much harm. Matt and Spence were camped on the blocks, and with Carlos and Isaiah at the top of the key, the chance of any of the girls making it into the paint was pretty slim anyway.

With the guys set up in a zone, Jenna had lots of options. Except driving into the key. She passed it to Emma, who faked a drive, turned when she ran up against Spence and passed it on to Chelsea. Chelsea passed it off to Carlotta, then into the corner where Amber was waiting. Amber went up for a jump shot that bounced off the rim.

I had to hand it to Noah. Matt and Spence were there. He could have left the rebound to them, but he jumped up and snatched it out of midair, looking so surprised I almost laughed out loud.

"Noah!" Carlos yelled.

Noah pivoted and spied Carlos near the half-court line, cutting for a fast break. He tried to do the right thing. He heaved the ball in Carlos's direction. What he hadn't taken into account was the speed of the defense. Or the fact that Carlos was already starting to run down the court. The ball bounced just short of Carlos, and before he could stop and backtrack, Emma swooped in, scooped it up and drove in for the layup. Two points.

I groaned. Stretch wasn't discouraged though. "That could have happened to anyone," he said. "Emma's quick."

I was curious to see how Stretch's offensive plan would work. It was unconventional. Usually when your team had the height advantage, you would go to the tall man for the shot. In this case, our tall man couldn't shoot. Some of the girls were almost as tall as Spence and Isaiah, so the guys might have a harder time getting past the defense than they thought.

Noah camped himself midway between the block and the free-throw line, ready to jump into the key. Chelsea manned up on him, but her six-foot height wasn't much compared to his six-foot-four, and you could see she wasn't taking him seriously anyway.

Carlos approached the three-point line and passed the ball back to Isaiah. I knew the girls expected Isaiah to drive in for a layup by the way they all closed in around him. Instead, he lobbed a pass over their heads to Noah. Chelsea was so surprised she barely twitched when Noah ducked around her. He passed the ball over to Spence, who was now wide open, and Spence put up the jump shot. Our lead was back to ten points.

"Yes!" shouted Stretch. "Good play, Noah!"

Noah ran back to midcourt, the grin on his face wider than the Grand Canyon.

Jenna called a time-out. She knew what was going on, and she needed to straighten her girls out.

Stretch used the time to give us a pep talk. *Keep up the good work, don't slack off*, that sort of thing. Then he subbed me in for Carlos, and we were back on court.

Now we had two tall players. That should be an advantage. We set up our zone and I watched as Jenna brought the ball down the court. I knew she'd have a game plan. I just didn't know what it was. She dribbled in close, faked a pass to Amber and then bounce-passed it to Emma, positioned between Spence and me. Emma put up a jump shot that went off the backboard. This time Noah wasn't quick enough. Chelsea charged in and grabbed the rebound. She went up for a second shot, and both Noah and I moved in to stop her.

The ref's whistle blew. "Foul on number 52, Blue."

A personal foul on Noah. I didn't know whether to be proud or disappointed. He'd never had enough confidence to get a foul before. It showed how much he'd improved. On the other hand, Chelsea now had two foul shots. And a good chance of getting them in.

The first one flew through the hoop with barely a whisper.

The second one wasn't quite so perfect. It hit the rim but dropped in the net after a couple of spins around the ring.

It was clear now that Jenna's strategy was to play on Noah's weaknesses. And she knew them inside out. On our next possession, Chelsea purposely fouled on Noah in the key. Of course, his free throws didn't have a hope of going in. The girls managed to get the rebound, brought it up the court and scored in about five seconds.

Stretch called a time-out to revise our strategy.

"We need to draw the defense away from Noah before passing to him," he said. "He has to avoid getting fouled at all costs." He didn't say it, but we all knew what he was thinking. We couldn't afford to let Noah take any free throws.

It meant drawing out the play to the full thirty-five seconds on the shot clock. A couple of times we barely got the shot before the buzzer. But we held them off fairly well, and when Noah was finally subbed off again, with five minutes left on the clock, the score was 60–55 our way. Yeah, they'd gained a bit of ground. Yeah, it hadn't been our best basketball as a team.

The important thing was we were still ahead, and Noah had proven that he could be an asset to the team.

The final minutes clocked out nicely. I think the girls knew they were done. Both teams scored a few more points, turned over the ball a couple of times and drew a ton of fouls in a desperate attempt to either get or maintain the lead. When the final buzzer sounded, the score was girls 62, boys 69, and the place went wild.

Chapter Seven

The game seemed to break the ice between Jenna and me—it's hard to resist a collective adrenaline rush. After the game everyone was on a high, and we hit Jo's diner with both Mountview teams and a good portion of the cheerleading squad, taking over a whole row of booths.

Jenna called Noah over to join us at a table with Amber, Carlotta and Stretch.

"Come on, let's take a picture," she said, squeezing over to make room for him.

It was a tight fit getting six basketball players into a booth meant for four normal-size people. He and Jenna and I leaned together, and she snapped a selfie with her phone.

"Nice moves out there tonight, Walker," she said after tucking her phone back into her pocket.

"Thanks," said Noah. I think he actually blushed. "You guys were awesome. We only won because of the height advantage."

Stretch cleared his throat loudly. "Let's not neglect to mention the fantastic coaching effort by yours truly."

"Yeah, that too." Noah paid Jo for his soda and gazed around the diner. It wasn't his usual hangout. The noise level was through the roof. With everyone pumped up on adrenaline and sugar, it sounded more like the school cafeteria than a restaurant. I felt sorry for the few customers who'd been in there before we arrived.

The noise didn't stop me from feeling the vibration in Jenna's pocket, though, telling her a message had arrived on her phone. We were packed in so tight I was surprised it didn't reverberate around the whole group. I glanced over at her, but she just ignored the phone and me.

"Did you see Emily Whitton got a new piercing?" said Amber, and the moment for me to ask Jenna about the call was gone.

"Another one?" said Jenna. "Does she have any body parts left to drill holes into? Where did she put this one?"

Amber scrunched up her nose. "In her breastbone."

Jenna gestured toward her chest and winced. "Like...?"

"Right between her boobs," said Amber, nodding.

I stopped listening. I didn't need to know any more about Emily Whitton or her piercings and especially not her body parts.

"How's the knee?" I asked Stretch. He'd been wearing a brace all week.

"Not as bad as I thought," said Stretch. "The X-rays were clear, so it's physio for a couple of weeks, and then I can get back to training."

"That's great," I said, although I couldn't help feeling a slight pang of anxiety in my stomach. If Stretch was cleared to play, would I be back on the bench for the rest of the playoffs?

"What do you think about the triangle offense?" I said.

Stretch shrugged. "It's a risk. But if we can pull it off, it may mean the difference between going to regionals and being satisfied with making the first round. It might be worth it, especially against a first draw like Columbia."

So he thought there was a chance Coach would run it in a game. I glanced over at Jenna to see if she'd heard that, but she was still deep in conversation with Amber and Carlotta.

Later, as we were waiting in the parking lot for Jenna's mom to pick her up, I mentioned to Jenna what Stretch had said.

"Really?" she said, taking her cell out of her pocket. She glanced at it and then went still.

"What's it say this time?" I said. She'd obviously seen the message that had come in earlier. And from her reaction, I could safely assume it was from the same bully who'd been bugging her before.

"Nothing," said Jenna. She glanced around the lot as if searching for something. Or someone.

A sudden thought gripped me. "Is that perv watching you?" I said, having a good look around too. Except for a couple of cars parked near the entrance to the restaurant, the lot looked deserted. "This is getting beyond creepy, Jenna. It's got to stop."

She didn't say anything.

"Why don't you block him on Facebook?" I said.

"I did," said Jenna. "I'm not totally stupid, you know."

"Then how...?"

"He's got my email address." Jenna looked up at me, and I could tell she was trying not to show how freaked out she was. "Someone must have given it to him."

My stomach clenched into a knot. "Who is this guy, Jenna? Do you know him? What does he want?"

Jenna sank down onto the curb, and I sat next to her. She seemed to make a decision, because suddenly her body relaxed a bit. "His name is Nick Smith, but I have no idea who he is. I looked at his profile, but I don't recognize him from anywhere."

I couldn't think of any Nick Smiths either, although there were a few Smith families in town. Mind you, a name like that could be an alias. He could easily have set up a Facebook account with a fake name. There were lots of creeps in the world. But why Jenna?

"What does he say in the messages?" I said. "What does he want?"

Jenna shrugged. "That's just it. He keeps saying things like *Keep your trap shut* and *If you say anything to anyone, we will hunt you down*."

The words chilled me. "We? So he's not in it alone."

"I guess not, but the problem is, I don't know what he wants me to keep quiet about," she said miserably.

"Have you asked?"

"Yes!" Jenna was clearly frustrated. "When I got the first threat, I messaged him back right away, asked who it was and what he wanted. I thought it was a prank or something."

"And...?"

"He said, *Don't play games with me. You know exactly what I'm talking about.* But I don't!"

I was confused. If the threats were real, and they seemed to be, why not spell it out? Tell Jenna what he wanted her to do? But then, maybe he didn't want to put anything in writing that could incriminate him later.

"Since then I've just been ignoring the messages, but maybe I should ask him again," said Jenna.

I shook my head emphatically. "No, don't respond to him, Jenna, or he'll know he's got to you. How long have the messages been coming? Could they be related to that robbery at the 7-Eleven a few weeks back?" Jenna and her cousin had been in the store just before it happened. I knew Jenna had been interviewed by the cops a couple of times.

"I don't see how," she said. "It's been almost four weeks since I got the first one, but that robbery was ages ago. And I didn't see anything anyway. Just a couple of guys crossing the parking lot as I got into Mel's car. I'd never be able to identify them or anything."

"But you gave the cops a description, right?" I said.

"Yeah, two guys in jeans. One in a gray hoodie, one in a leather jacket. That could be just about any guy in town."

It didn't seem enough to warrant stalking Jenna. Because that's all you could call it. *Cyberbullying* seemed like too soft a word.

"And now someone has given him your email address?"

Jenna nodded.

"That means someone you know knows him," I said, thinking out loud. "Have you asked around?"

"No." Jenna turned to look at me. "And don't go spreading it around, Dylan. That's the whole point. I've got to keep quiet. If I keep quiet, nothing will happen, and he'll go away."

Lights flashed at the entrance to the parking lot, and Jenna's mom's car turned in.

"Please, Dylan," she said. "Promise me you won't say anything to anyone."

Her mom stopped the car in front of us.

Jenna gave me a pleading look. The one I can never resist.

"Okay," I said. "But promise me you'll tell me if he contacts you again."

"I will," she said, all smiles. She put her arms around me and squeezed me tightly.

"And see if you can get him blocked on your email," I said. "You should be able to change your settings to do that."

She nodded. "See you Monday," she said and hopped into the car.

Chapter Eight

As it turned out, I didn't see Jenna on Monday. She wasn't at school. When she didn't reply to my text before first period, I started to panic. What if something had happened to her? What if that guy had followed through on his threats? What if she was lying dead in a ditch somewhere, or tied up in a dark basement? By the end of English, I was ready to go to the police right then and there.

Lucky for me, I got a reply just as I was gathering up my stuff.

I'm fine. Just a stomach bug. Don't panic.

Thanks for letting me know, I replied, angry. **I was worried.**

Nothing to worry about. Don't come over. You don't want to catch this before the game on Wed.

As the adrenaline surge waned and my heart started to slow down, I thought about how stupid I would have looked had the cops showed up at Jenna's house to investigate a missing person only to find her with her head in the toilet. Still attached to her body. But it also made me think about how I would feel if something did happen to Jenna and I'd done nothing to help her. I'd never be able to forgive myself. *Someone* knew Nick Smith. *Someone* had supplied him with Jenna's email address. There had to be a way to find out who that was without asking every kid in school.

Just then Noah walked by and ducked into the computer-science lab. A lightbulb went on in my head. If anyone could find the culprit who was feeding Nick Smith information about Jenna, it was Noah. He knew just about everything there was to know about computers. And once we found the link between Jenna and that creep, we'd have a better idea of what we were dealing with. I had promised Jenna I wouldn't tell anyone what was happening, but I wouldn't have to tell Noah everything. And if we did find out who this guy was and what he was doing, she'd forget all about that promise.

I tracked Noah down at lunch.

"Noah. Can I talk to you for a minute?"

"If it's about another extra practice this afternoon, I can't make it," he said. "We've got debating finals coming up next week, and we have to prepare our persuasive argument and points for our rebuttal."

I didn't even know what that meant. "No, it's not that," I said, looking around for a place to talk that wasn't swarming with kids.

I dragged him into an empty classroom.

"What's going on?" said Noah.

"I need some advice. I'm trying to find someone," I said. "Or at least find out stuff about him."

"So google him," said Noah.

"That's just it. His name's Nick Smith. If I google him, I'll get, like, a million hits," I said. Actually, I hadn't even thought about googling him. I'd do that when I got home. "All I know is, he has a Facebook account."

"How do you know he's got an account?" said Noah.

Here's where it got a bit tricky. "He sent me a message," I said. I'd decided I'd just keep Jenna's name out of the conversation. Noah didn't need to know who the guy was sending messages to. "I had a look at his profile pic, but I didn't recognize him." At least, Jenna had.

"So friend him. Then you'll be able to see his full profile. You can always unfriend him if he's not the guy you think he is."

"Well, here's the thing," I said. I was treading on very thin ice now. "The message he sent wasn't exactly friendly. I don't want to open myself up to some stalker or something."

"Someone's threatening you?" he said.

"Not exactly," I said evasively.

"It's a no-brainer, Dylan. They call it cyberbullying, remember? Go to Mr. Anderson or the counselor," said Noah. It was like hearing a delayed echo. I'd said exactly those words to Jenna only last week. "It's probably someone at school who set up an account with a fake name. Don't cave in to a bully, online or not."

"I can't go to Mr. Anderson," I said.

"Why not? Once it's out in the open, it'll stop. Keeping it secret is what keeps it going." Noah was getting pretty worked up. This was obviously a sensitive topic for him. "Dylan," he said. "It's nothing to be ashamed of. Anyone can be a victim of cyberbullying. It doesn't mean anything. It doesn't make you any less of a man."

Okay, this was going too far.

"It's not me," I blurted out. "It's Jenna."

He couldn't have looked more shocked if I'd slapped him.

"And I promised her I wouldn't tell anyone."

"Oh." Noah swallowed.

I explained what had been happening. "So someone knows this guy and has given him Jenna's email address," I finished. "The little weasel."

Noah pulled his laptop out from under his books and started it. I'd never seen him so worked up. He was usually Mr. Calm. It made me wonder if he had more experience in this area than he was letting on. He wasn't exactly Mr. Popular. But then, Jenna *was* popular, and look what was happening to her.

"What are you doing?" I asked.

"Checking out Jenna's Facebook friends," he said.

"None of her friends would give some creep her email address," I said.

"Not knowingly," said Noah. He was flicking through profiles faster than I could follow. "But if one of them gave her email address to another friend, and that friend gave it to someone else who knew our mysterious Nick Smith..."

I was beginning to get where he was going with this. It was like an online version of a rumor passing through the school from one kid to another. The information always ended up in the wrong hands.

"That someone is bound to be Facebook friends with Mr. Smith, and if we can find out who that is..." He continued to flick through profiles, going from one friend to another in the blink of an eye.

"This might take a while," he said. "Get on another computer and start checking out the friends of Jenna's friends. See if Nick Smith is friends with any of them. Start with her closest friends. The ones who would have her email address. Don't bother looking at your own profile. I'm already onto that."

I was about to protest that I would never give Jenna's email address to the wrong person when I realized the futility of it. The whole point of a rumor mill was that it went from one trusted hand to another. Until it ended up in the wrong hands.

"Got it," said Noah half an hour later. I'd almost gotten to the point of giving up. Jenna had a lot of friends. And her friends had a lot of friends. Every profile hop expanded the pool of names exponentially.

I spun around and looked over Noah's shoulder at the screen.

Nick Smith. He looked about twenty-five. Dark brown hair, a bit scruffy-looking. His profile photo looked like it was taken in some bar. I'd never seen him in my life.

"How did you find him?" I asked. "Who's the jerk who gave him Jenna's email address?"

"Jesse Derby."

"What?" I was shocked. Okay, I'll admit I knew next to nothing about Jesse. He never hung out with the rest of us. Always left practice or a game before anyone else had stepped foot out of the locker room. He often skipped practices—and classes, too, for that matter. But he was still a teammate. I felt betrayed.

"We don't actually have any proof that he gave this guy Jenna's email address," said Noah, always more levelheaded than me. "All we know is that he's Facebook friends with him."

"Well, I'm going to find out," I said. I had a burning sensation in my chest. I wanted to punch something.

Noah grabbed my arm and pulled me back into my chair. "Just relax and put your brain back in gear for a minute," he said. "We don't want to make things worse for Jenna."

That settled me down a bit. "No, you're right," I said. I still felt like I had smoke coming out of my ears, but the fire had reduced to a smoulder.

"Let's talk to Jenna. See if she knows this guy," he said.

"She doesn't," I said. "She's certain she's never seen him before. The only one who knows this guy is Jesse Derby." The last two words came out as a growl.

"Still, knowing the connection between him and Jesse may jog her memory. If we can figure out why he's trying to scare her, we can talk her into going to the cops. Threatening someone online has criminal consequences, you know."

I didn't like it, but I knew he was right. "Okay," I said.

Chapter Nine

I had a hard time being around Jesse at practice the next morning. The way he ran around on the court, passing and dribbling like nothing had happened. Like it was an ordinary day and his buddy wasn't making death threats to my girlfriend. I wanted to wipe the smug look off his face with the back of my hand.

After forty-five minutes of running drills, Coach set us up for some one-on-one shooting practice. I scooted over to Jesse and gave him a friendly grin. Not.

It was an unusual choice, and Jesse knew it. Normally, I would have paired up with Matt or Carlos, or Stretch, before he hurt his knee. I think Jesse may have sensed something was up. Still, he shrugged and started dribbling the ball. He eyed me warily as he shuffled from one side to the other. Perhaps he could see the murderous intent behind my smile. Perhaps he just knew I was the better player. Either way, he was taking his time making any moves.

He glanced up at the hoop, and I thought he might just go for the long-range shot. Coach wouldn't have been happy about that. It was the cop-out move. We could practice long-range shots any time. Then suddenly he switched hands and turned his back to me, sidestepping closer to the basket. I matched him stride for stride, left, right, left again and forward, letting him herd me into position. When he spun and drove in for the layup, I made my own move.

I stepped in, crossed my arms and bumped him. Hard.

Jesse reeled back and hit the floor.

"What the—?"

"Whoa, sorry about that," I said, giving him a hand up. I would rather have given a hand up to Hitler, but I had to keep up appearances. "Let's go again."

He gave me a guarded look and started dribbling again, keeping an eye on me while he switched the ball from his right hand to his left and back again.

"Come on, don't take all day," I said, gesturing for him to come closer.

He faked to the left, then drove in past me on the right.

I turned and jumped as he went for the layup. We collided in midair, and both of us hit the floor.

"What the hell is wrong with you?" he said as he got to his feet.

"What?" I said innocently. "I'm defending the basket. What does it look like?"

He scowled at me. I almost thought he was going to walk off the court, but he got to the top of the key and turned back, prepared for another attempt. This time he drove straight in. I rushed right at him, and he hit the floor for the third time.

He jumped up, anger written all over him. With a glance over his shoulder to make sure Coach wasn't watching, he stepped up and got right into my face.

"I don't know what your problem is, Lane, but you're asking for it," he said.

"Yeah?" I growled back. "What're you gonna do about it? Get your buddy to send me nasty emails?" The words were out before I could stop them. I could have kicked myself.

Jesse's eyes widened, then his brows drew down in feigned confusion.

"I don't know what you're talking about," he said, stepping back. "You're nuts." He turned and jogged toward the other end of the court. "Walker! Switch with me," he called out. "Lane's lost his marbles."

"Are you stupid?" Noah said when I told him what had happened. "Isn't this exactly what we didn't want?"

"I know," I said. "Shut up about it, all right? I feel bad enough already. Just help me figure out what to do."

"We've got to talk to Jenna," he said. "Now."

"She's home with the stomach flu," I said.

"Then we'll just have to go out there."

I couldn't argue. Both of us knew how serious this was.

My car was still at the body shop, so Noah drove us out to Jenna's after school. He was driving a king-cab Nissan Frontier that still smelled like a new car.

"Your dad lets you drive this?" I asked, looking around appreciatively. "It looks brand new."

"It is. And it's not his," Noah said.

"You bought this? Where'd you get that kind of money?"

Noah shrugged. "It's an early graduation present," he said.

I whistled. I'd known Noah's family was pretty well-off. His dad was one of the local doctors, and his mom owned a dress shop in Vancouver. I hadn't realized how well-off.

Going around Devil's Bend reminded me again of the car accident. Debris and tire marks were still visible around the accident site. Suddenly, I wondered if there was a connection between the two—the accident and the threatening messages. The cops had never found the black pickup. Could it belong to Nick Smith?

When Jenna saw us at the door, she was pretty upset. I don't know if it was just us or the effects of the stomach bug. Even as she opened the door, she looked pale and scared, like she was on the verge of tears.

"You told Noah?" she asked me accusingly. "Dyl, you promised."

"Jenna, we got something," I said. "Nick Smith is Facebook friends with Jesse Derby."

She calmed down a little when she heard that. "Jesse Derby, from your team?" she said. "I've never even spoken to him."

Noah brought Nick's profile up on his laptop, and we gathered around to have a look.

"Does that help at all? Do you recognize him now?" Noah asked.

Jenna shook her head. "No. I've never seen him before. Not that I remember anyway."

We flicked through Nick's profile, but it didn't give us much beyond putting a face to the name. The guy's privacy settings were high, so we couldn't see any of his posts. The only Facebook friend we recognized was Jesse Derby, which confirmed our suspicions that Jesse had given Nick Jenna's email address but didn't give us any new information. It looked like we were coming up with a big fat zero.

"Do you think Jesse gave this guy my email address?" asked Jenna.

"He's the only connection with you we've found," said Noah.

"Why would he do that?" said Jenna.

"That's another mystery," said Noah, closing his computer. "Has this guy sent you any more messages?"

Jenna swallowed and nodded. I knew it was bad news.

"What? What's happened now?" I said.

"I did like you said and found a way to block his emails," she said. "That was on Monday. Today the messages started coming in on my phone. Text messages. He's got my cell number."

Noah and I looked at each other. We both knew what the other was thinking. Jesse Derby. It had to be.

"Can we see them?" asked Noah.

Jenna got her phone from the other room and flicked to the messages section. "It's not just messages," she said. "There are photos too. He's been following me."

I looked at the string of photos, and fear gripped my insides. There were photos of Jenna outside the school, at the rec center, at Jo's diner, getting into my car, walking down the street with Amber. The last one was of her house.

"He's been sending them almost every hour," she said.

"You have to go to the police," said Noah. "This is outright stalking."

"No!" she said. "He's made it clear. No police. If I just stay quiet, nothing will happen."

"But quiet about what?" I said. "How can you keep quiet if you don't know what to keep quiet about?"

"I don't know," Jenna snapped. "He won't tell me, remember? Thinks I'm just playing dumb. Keeping quiet is the only thing I can do right now. Just leave it alone."

She sighed. I could see how stressed and worried she was about this. I wanted to put my arms around her and tell her everything would be okay. But when I went to give her a hug, she backed up, putting out her hand to ward me off.

"You guys better get out of here before you end up with my stomach flu," she said, trying to smile. "You've got to be fit for the game tomorrow."

I wasn't happy about it, but we left.

Noah paused at the door. "Don't delete those photos, Jenna. Or any other messages he's sent you. It's the only evidence we have."

On the way back to town, I told Noah about the car accident and how we'd been run off the road by the black pickup.

"Yeah, I saw Jenna's Facebook post," he said.

"Do you think the driver of the truck could have been Nick Smith?" I said.

He glanced over at me. "It's a definite possibility. Is that when Jenna started getting those messages?"

"No, it was before that." And that meant the messages couldn't have been a result of her posting that call for information about the black pickup. It still seemed like too much of a coincidence though. Jenna starts getting threatening messages. Then someone deliberately tries to run me off the road. What if it hadn't been some random act of road rage? What if it was another attempt to intimidate Jenna? A very real, very dangerous attempt to show her he meant business? The thought was enough to give me goose bumps.

We drove along in silence for a few miles, and then Noah spoke up.

"There might be a way we can find out more about this guy," he said.

"What?"

"Well, Jesse Derby is friends with him. If we get into Jesse's account, we'll be able to see everything this Nick Smith has posted."

"There's no way Jesse Derby is going to let us into his account," I said. "That's practically admitting he helped this guy stalk Jenna."

Noah kept his eyes on the road. "I wasn't thinking of asking Jesse," he said grimly.

We stopped in at Jo's Diner and holed up in a booth at the back. The after-school crowd had pretty much vacated the place, and no one paid any attention to us.

Noah brought up the Facebook login page. "All we need is his email address and password," he said.

Yeah, like it was that easy, I thought.

"Coach sent us a group email at the beginning of the season with the game schedule," Noah said. "So the email address is easy." He found the email and cut and pasted Jesse's address into the Facebook login. "Come to think of it," he said, "that may be how Jesse got Jenna's email address too. Getting the girls' schedule forwarded from someone on her team." He shrugged.

"Now for the password." Noah turned to me. "Jesse doesn't seem like the kind of guy who's really picky about his passwords, so what do you know about him?"

I shrugged. "Not much."

"Come on, think," he said. "Pets? Birthdays? Girlfriends? Nicknames?"

"I don't know." I tried to think of everything I knew about Jesse Derby. It wasn't much. "He's got a picture of Guns N' Roses in his locker," I said. Carlos's locker was two doors down from his. I'd seen that poster hundreds of times.

"Guns' N' Roses." He punched it in, but a message saying *invalid password* came up. Then he tried AxlRose.

"What's AxlRose?" I asked.

"The lead singer," said Noah. The same message came up again.

"Do you listen to Guns N' Roses?" I asked, curious. It wasn't a band I would have thought Noah would be into.

He shrugged. "I listen to lots of stuff. Now what else? And make it good. We may not get too many chances at this before we're locked out."

I thought. "I think he has a dog," I said. "But I have no idea what its name is."

"What kind of a dog?" said Noah.

"Like, a Rottweiler or a bull mastiff or something," I said. I'd seen him with it down at the park across from the school. It wasn't the kind of dog I'd want to mess with.

Noah tried various names—Butch, Rocky, Spike, Gunner, Atlas, Rebel, Princess. All invalid.

"Princess?" I asked.

"Some people have a weird sense of humor," said Noah.

"Wait," I said, suddenly remembering. "Back in elementary school, Jesse had a birthday party. I remember because it was right before Christmas, and we all thought it wasn't fair that he'd get presents on Christmas Eve and on Christmas morning too. His birthday is December 24."

I also remembered that party because of the way it had ended. We'd been kicking a ball around in the backyard, as kids do. Jesse kicked it toward a kid named Alex Murphy and it flew wild, hitting Jesse's dad and making him spill his beer. I'd never seen anyone hit the roof as fast as Richard Derby did that day. He went agro on Jesse, and we all left pretty quickly. It was the first and last party I remember Jesse having.

"Okay, that's good," said Noah. "122497." It was too much to hope for, but I couldn't help feeling disappointed when *invalid password* came up yet again. "Or maybe Dec2497," said Noah.

A new message appeared. *Security check.* We were given a letter-and-number code to type in. Noah copied it carefully, and we were back to the login page.

"Okay, we've got to get it now," said Noah. "I doubt they're going to let us try much longer."

But we'd come to a dead end. I couldn't think of a single further bit of information about Jesse Derby. Nothing that he'd use for a password. Would we ever find Nick Smith? I stared at the computer, wishing it would somehow transmit Jesse's password to me by computer telepathy.

"Hold on," I said. "What was that date you put in?"

"122497," said Noah.

"Not 97," I said. "Try 96. Jesse was ten the year of the party. A year older than me."

Noah plugged in the numbers, and we held our breath.

The login worked.

"You did it!" I said.

"No, you did it," said Noah, already scrolling through Jesse's friends to find

Nick Smith. I have to admit to a twinge of guilt about hacking into Jesse's account. It lasted about half a second, until Noah clicked the screen one more time and we were face to face with Nick Smith's full profile. The guy who was threatening Jenna. With Jesse's assistance.

Nick Smith's bio claimed that he lived in Vancouver, Washington. No surprise there. It was only an hour away. He was married to Leanne Smith and had two kids. And he worked at a Ford dealership. I could believe that. He looked sleazy enough to be a car salesman. And that could explain the brand-new Ford F-150, if it did belong to him.

We scrolled down through his posts, hoping to find something from around the time he started sending messages to Jenna. Nothing jumped out at us. It was all the usual stuff. And there were no black pickups in his photos either. So with all that we had gone through to hack into Jesse's account, we were no closer to finding out what Nick wanted with Jenna. Or whether he'd been the driver of the black pickup. I wasn't just disappointed. I was devastated.

"Let me check Jesse's messages," said Noah. "See if he contacted Nick privately." But there were no messages there at all, so either Jesse didn't use Facebook for messaging or he'd deleted them all.

"All that and nothing," I said. "Not even a photo with the truck in it. What's wrong with this guy? Who doesn't put up a photo of his car?"

Noah closed the laptop and sat back in the booth. "There is another way to find out if Nick Smith drives a black pickup," he said.

He had a funny smile on his face that rekindled a grain of hope in me. "What are you thinking?" I asked. I was beginning to see there was more to Noah Walker than brains.

"Feel like a drive into Vancouver?" he said.

Nick and Leanne Smith lived on the east side of the city. Their address was easy to find in the white pages. According to Google Maps, it would only take us an hour and ten minutes to get there. We grabbed a couple of burgers to go and headed off.

It was dark by the time we drove down 164th Avenue, looking for the turnoff. Passing by a few large apartment complexes, it suddenly dawned on me that Nick Smith probably had a garage. And if he used that garage, we would never know what kind of car he drove, and it would all be for nothing.

"This is it," said Noah, turning down a side street. "Keep an eye out for number 14450."

The burger seemed to turn over in my stomach as I scanned the houses. It was hard to see the house numbers in the dark. A few people had porch lights on, though, and we glimpsed enough numbers to know roughly where we were.

"That was 14440," I said. "It must be just up there."

Noah pulled over opposite the house at 14450. It was a smallish house, probably a rental. The yard was kind of overgrown, and the fence was in need of repairs. There was a light on in the front room, and I could see shadows moving behind the curtains. The driveway was empty.

The disappointment was sharp in my throat.

"It was a long shot," said Noah.

"Yeah."

"What do you want to do now?"

"Go back, I guess," I said. "It's not like we can knock on the door and say, 'Did you run me off the road with a black pickup last week?'"

"No, I guess not."

We sat there for a couple of minutes longer. Neither of us had any other ideas, and finally Noah started up the engine. "The truck needed a good run to break it in, anyway," he said.

He did a U-turn and headed back the way we had come. We'd only gone a block down the road when headlights appeared up ahead, and a vehicle drove past us.

"That's it!" I shouted. "That was it. Turn around."

Noah did another U-ey and pulled over a few houses down from 14450. We watched as a man got out of a black Ford F-150 and reached behind the seat to grab a bag. He slung it over his shoulder and went into the house, pausing on the front porch to lock the vehicle with a *beep* and a flash of lights. As he passed under the porch light, I recognized him from his Facebook profile. It was definitely Nick Smith.

Noah and I got out of the Frontier. We crossed the road and casually walked past the house. I took a good look at the back bumper of the pickup as we passed, then dug my phone out of my pocket and took a couple of photos. The right-hand corner was dented and scratched, and I was sure that in daylight, I would have seen streaks of silver paint from my Honda.

Chapter Ten

Game day dawned clear and cold. To say I was distracted would have been an understatement. With everything we had learned in the past couple of days, it was hard to concentrate on basketball. Especially when we loaded ourselves onto the bus and headed down the same road to Vancouver that Noah and I had driven the night before.

We'd decided to keep quiet about what we'd found out for now. Nick Smith obviously meant business, and we didn't want to do anything to set him off. Until we found out why he was targeting Jenna and what he wanted her to keep quiet about, we'd just have to lay low.

Columbia's gymnasium was already crowded with spectators. As the higher-ranked team, they had the home-court advantage, and I could see it was going to work in their favor. We'd brought as many supporters as the bus would hold, including Stretch and our cheerleading team, but they were vastly outnumbered by the Columbia fans. The team mascot, a large brown bear, was already pacing the sidelines, winding the crowd up. Seeing the masses of kids and parents swarming over the bleachers, I wondered just for a second if Nick Smith was up there. But it was Jenna whom Nick Smith was watching. And Jenna was still at home sick. So if Nick was anywhere, it was camped outside her house. That thought gave me a queasy feeling in my stomach, and I sent Jenna a quick text.

About to start the game. Wish me luck.

I was relieved when she texted back straightaway. **Good luck. Wish I was there. xx**

Coach Scott called us into a huddle and gave us our final instructions. There wasn't too much he could say. We'd gone over our opening game plan so many times the day before in practice, it had been running through my head like a bad song.

"This is our chance," he said. "Mountview hasn't been in the playoffs for over ten years. You guys have what it takes. You can win this thing. So go hard, play fair, and remember our game plan."

"Hunters!"

We ran onto the court.

The Columbia center was tall and lean. Stretch would have been a good match for him. He gave me a smile that basically said, "Go your hardest, shrimp," and I glared back at him. There was no way I would let him think he could intimidate me. Even if he was pretty intimidating.

The ref tossed the ball up, and the Columbia giant got the tip. We were off and running.

The plan was to start out with a 2-1-2 zone defense. Coach had done his research on Columbia, and long-range shooting seemed to be their weak spot. We needed to keep them out of the key. Force them to take the long shots. It was a risk. If they got the long shots in, those three-pointers could add up pretty quickly. But this wasn't the time for playing things safe. We wanted to win, not give ourselves a pat on the back at the end for putting in a good show in the first round.

The strategy worked well. For about ten minutes. We managed to keep them out of the key, and while they got some buckets, Coach had been right. Their long-range percentage wasn't that great. Isaiah was on fire, scoring basket after basket. Ten minutes into the game, we were up 18–11, and we were feeling pretty good. That's when their coach called a time-out and subbed in number 61.

He wasn't big, he wasn't super fast, but he could shoot. If this had been baseball, you would have called him the pinch hitter. Our zone, which had been working so well up until now, was totally useless. They brought the ball down, passed it around a bit until number 61 came open, and then up he went with the jump shot. They'd closed the gap to three points when Coach called our own time-out.

"Time for a new game plan," he said. "Half-court man defense. Derby, you're on for Zuckerman. Man up on 61. And Walker, you're on for Lane."

"What?" The word came out of my mouth before I could stop it. He was putting Noah on now?

"You're off your game, Dylan," said Coach. "I don't know what you've got on your mind, but if you put on a man defense like I saw yesterday at practice, you'll be giving away free throws, and we can't afford that."

The whistle blew, and Spence and I hit the bench.

"Tough break," said Stretch sympathetically.

I couldn't believe Coach had pulled me off. A three-point lead in a playoff game and Coach subbed on Noah Walker? He must have hit his head on the way to the game.

Noah looked small next to the Columbia center. Small and weak. In actual fact, Noah's taller than I am, but his lack of confidence took about three inches off him. The center could see that straightaway and gave Noah a little bump and a grin. Noah grinned back. He looked like he was going to be sick.

Jesse passed the ball in to Carlos, and he brought it up the court, nice and slow. Columbia had set up a zone, probably to stop Isaiah driving into the key. Carlos passed it off to Matt, who fired it straight to Isaiah. Only there was nowhere for Isaiah to go. He stood there, dribbling on the spot, trying to decide on the best move. I knew the play he should make. Pass it on to the center standing on the block, draw the defense away, then duck into the key and be ready for the pass back. The problem was, the center on the block was Noah, not me or Stretch.

Isaiah made his decision. He passed it back to Matt. Matt dribbled it twice, faked a pass to Jesse, then went for the jump shot.

The shot bounced off the rim. Noah dived into the key for the rebound, but he was no match for Columbia's center. The Columbia giant grabbed it, spun and passed it off before his feet even hit the ground.

Columbia's guard caught it and took off down the court. Matt was onto him in a flash, but the guy switched hands, spun, and passed it off to number 14, standing at the top of the key. I thought he would go for the shot, forgetting that long-range shots weren't their strong point. Instead, he drove in for the layup. Isaiah set his block, and the guy plowed straight into him.

The ref's whistle blew. Yes! Charging foul.

"Blocking foul. Number 8, Mountview. Two shots."

I jumped to my feet. Blocking foul? On Isaiah?

"No way!" I said. "He set the block. It's charging."

Coach waved me back into my seat. I could see he agreed with me. There was nothing he could do, though, without risking a technical foul.

While the teams set up for the free throws, the Columbia coach subbed off their center. I think he'd figured out Noah wasn't a threat and was taking the opportunity to rest his best center for the second half. The sub was no bigger than Noah, but he had the same wolfish grin as his teammate, and Noah looked just as intimidated.

The shooter bounced the ball a couple of times, took aim and let off the first shot. It hit the backboard and dropped through the net.

The ref passed him the ball again, and everyone set up for the rebound. Noah was doing the right thing—crouching, ready to jump in as soon as the shot was off. But I could see the Columbia center nudging him over, jostling for position. By the time the ball was released, Noah didn't have a chance in hell of getting it.

The ball bounced off the rim and everyone leaped for the rebound. Noah was a split second behind everyone else.

Enough for the Columbia center to reach up and grab the ball. He brought it down, bounced it and went to pop it up again. Matt was there. The center had nowhere to go. He turned and passed it off to number 23, who dribbled a couple of times and passed it to number 61.

I had to admit, I might not like Jesse Derby, but right now I could appreciate his street-thug attitude. He was in that guy's face, and he wasn't going anywhere. Number 61 couldn't get his shot off. He took it down into a dribble and tried to get away, but Jesse shadowed his every move. In the end, he passed it back out to number 23, who tried for the three-pointer and missed.

Matt got the rebound that time and fired it out to Carlos. It was exactly the move I would have made. Carlos tore down the court and passed it to Isaiah, who drove in for the layup.

I breathed a sigh of relief. It had worked out okay, but the fact was, Noah was out there doing nothing to help the team.

He wasn't getting the rebounds, and the guys didn't have enough confidence in him to pass him the ball. Not that I blamed them. He was playing like the old Noah again.

"Come on, Walker, man up!" shouted Coach.

"Noah," I yelled. "You know you're better than that. Get out there and play!" He'd proved it when we'd played the girls' team on Saturday night. He'd gained confidence that night, and it had shown in his game. He'd gotten better and better as the night went on. Was it the fact that he'd been playing girls? Jenna's team was good. We all knew that. In fact, they had a lot of skills the Columbia guys were lacking. But were girls ever as intimidating as these big guys?

"He's like Chelsea!" I yelled to Noah as he ran past. "Call him Chelsea."

Coach gave me a strange look, but Spence knew what I was getting at.

"Yeah, come on, Noah," he called out. "If we can beat the girls, we can beat these guys. Find your player!"

Noah didn't look our way. There was a change in his stance, though, that made me think he'd heard us. Suddenly he looked more solid, his steps more purposeful.

Noah camped himself in the key like he'd done on Saturday night. It wasn't exactly the man defense Coach had asked for, but pretty close. The Columbia center was hovering around the basket, looking for the pass, and Noah wedged himself in front of him whenever he could. When the center did get free for the pass, he turned and found Noah standing right in front of him. He faked a shot and passed it off again.

Coach glanced over at us again. "I don't even want to guess what all that Chelsea nonsense was about, but it's working," he said.

I grinned. It was the closest we'd get to a thank-you from Coach. As far as he was concerned, team motivation was all part of the game.

Matt intercepted a pass and threw the ball to Jesse, who took it halfway down the court before being trapped by his defender. Jesse paused, dribbling on the spot, looking for the open man.

"Noah's open!" I yelled.

Jesse glanced at him, then tried to pass it to Carlos.

Carlos's defender jumped in and tapped it away. The loose ball bounced toward the sideline before Matt and Isaiah and two of the Columbia defenders jumped on it.

The ref's whistle blew. "Jump ball!" He glanced toward the possession arrow. "Mountview's possession."

I threw my hands up. "Noah was open," I said. "He should have passed it to Noah."

"Don't worry about it," Stretch said, pulling me back onto the bench. "It's our possession anyway."

I scowled at Jesse as he ran past. "Lucky for him," I muttered.

Isaiah took the ball on the sideline. He waited, searching for the open man, but Jesse was on the other side of the key, ready for the inbounds pass and a chance at the basket, and Carlos and Matt couldn't get free from the Columbia defenders. Isaiah faked a couple of times in Matt's direction, then seemed to make up his mind. He lobbed the ball toward the key, straight into Noah's hands.

Noah looked surprised.

"Shoot!" I yelled. "Shoot it, Noah!"

He panicked. The ball went up and straight over the basket to the other side without touching the hoop, the net or the backboard. Luckily, Jesse was there. He popped it back up and it bounced off the rim.

I felt like covering my eyes.

The Columbia center caught the rebound. Noah stood his ground, but the center pivoted and fired the pass off to another teammate.

Five seconds later they'd scored.

The halftime buzzer sounded, and we headed for the locker room.

Noah was pretty bummed. He knew he'd blown it in those final seconds. But then, I was the one who'd told him to shoot, knowing he was crap at shooting.

"You did all right, Walker," said Coach. "Let's just leave the shooting to the other guys, shall we?"

Noah nodded, a sheepish grin on his face. He and I both knew he shouldn't have attempted that shot.

"Sorry, Noah," I said. "I thought it was worth a try."

He shrugged.

I heard the music start up for the Columbia cheerleaders' halftime routine. We sat around complaining about the other team and guzzling our drinks. Even Noah was getting in on the team bashing, which was a first for him. Stretch was talking earnestly to Coach Scott near the door to the bathroom. Jesse Derby was the only one who kept himself apart from the team. He sat in the corner, doing something on his phone. I couldn't help wondering if he was checking in with Nick Smith.

"All right, guys," said Coach when it was almost time for the second half. "Derby, you stay on number 61. Lane, you're on for Garth. Zuckerman, you sub on for Noble."

That left Noah and Carlos still on. Carlos had already played the whole first half. I didn't know how much he'd have left in him if he didn't get subbed off soon.

"We're going for a modified 2-3 defense," Coach continued. "Set up the zone, but Noah and Dylan, you close it up if anyone gets near the paint."

We nodded.

"I want a 3-out, 2-in offense. If you pass in to Walker, get ready for the pass out again. Dylan, look to shoot if you can, or kick it back to the perimeter."

We had run this offense in practice a million times, but never with this particular group. Usually, the post players were Matt and me. Now it was Noah and me, with Spence, Carlos and Jesse positioned around the three-point line. It should work. In theory. But somehow theory never seems to quite translate to reality.

We managed to keep their scoring percentage down by stopping number 61 from making the long-range shots and shutting down the lane. Unfortunately, our scoring percentage came down too. With Isaiah on the bench and Noah passing back out from the paint instead of shooting, that left Carlos, Spence and me to get the baskets. It was tough going. The scores on both sides crawled upward, until Columbia managed to creep past us at the ten-minute mark.

Despite the slow progress, Coach seemed satisfied with the play. Perhaps that was his intention all along. Slow everything down, give Carlos a break, and then go for the kill in the final push. I'm sure he hadn't intended for Columbia to get up, but it was only by two points. The way the crowd roared when they drew ahead, you would have thought they'd won the whole championship.

Coach called a time-out.

"Back to the original five," he said. "We're running the triangle offense."

It wasn't unexpected. In the back of my mind, I'd known it was coming. Still, my heart skipped a beat. It was a risk. It could also be our salvation.

"You know the drill," he said. "Take your lead from the ball handler. Your next move depends on what he does. React accordingly."

"Hunters!"

It was our ball, and we set up our triangle as soon as Carlos started bringing the ball upcourt. Columbia stuck with their man defense, which was all right with us. We could string them out, open up the space to make a move. It was up to Carlos to decide what that move would be.

Whoever said practice makes perfect is right. We'd been practicing this offense every day for the last week, and suddenly everything clicked into place. The ball went from Carlos to Matt to Isaiah, each player rotating position depending on who had the ball. Isaiah faked a drive to the basket, then passed it off to Matt, who went for the inside jump shot. The ball bounced off the rim, and I grabbed it and dunked it in. It was that easy. Well, not easy at all, actually, but it sure felt good.

The Columbia center didn't look quite so confident now. He tried his intimidation bump and grin on me again as their guard brought the ball down the court, but it lacked any true malice. A pass into the paint, and I knocked it away. Isaiah picked up the loose ball. We were on the offense again, racing down the court. Isaiah was held up in the key, and he passed the ball to Spence on the perimeter. Back to Isaiah again, on the corner now, then out to Carlos. Carlos drove in, spun and fired it to Matt. Up went the jump shot for a three.

We were in the zone. Columbia started getting desperate and gave away free throws, clocking up the fouls. The crowd was strangely quiet.

When the final buzzer sounded, the score was 58-49. We'd done it, and with a convincing win. No one would ever be able to say we didn't deserve to be in the playoffs now.

Chapter Eleven

It was the upset win of the season, and we were on a high the whole way back to school on the bus. Coach kept yelling at us to keep it down, but I don't think the noise got below the level of a jet engine in the hour it took us to get back to town. When we unloaded in front of the school, a few of the guys headed off to Jo's Diner. I needed to talk to Jenna.

She answered on the fifth ring. "Hey, congratulations," she said.

"You should have seen us, Jenna. We were on fire. And Noah. I've never seen him play like that. Ever."

"That's great," she said. "Did he score?"

I laughed. "No, I'm afraid you owe the team a round of sodas."

She laughed with me. "I hope Carlos will take a rain check," she said.

Suddenly, the world spun back into reality. "Why? Aren't you coming to school tomorrow?"

She hesitated. "No. Mom wants me to stay home one more day." Her voice sounded funny when she said it.

"This isn't because of those messages, is it?" I said.

"Of course not," she said quickly. "I've been really sick, Dylan. You know how protective my parents are."

"Yeah, sure," I said, not convinced at all. "Look, I get my car back tomorrow. Can I come out and see you?"

"Sure. That would be great," she said.

"See you tomorrow then."

Paying the bill to get my car back hurt. A lot. I'd had to borrow money from my dad, and the way I was going, I'd probably still be paying him back when I finished college. It was nice having wheels again though. I was done with walking.

On the way to Jenna's, I decided not to tell her about Nick Smith being the guy with the black pickup. She was freaked out enough already. It wouldn't change anything if I told her. We would still be in the same position, not knowing why he was intimidating her. And that was the key. We needed to find out what Jenna had done that he thought was so threatening to him.

I had a good look around the area on the way to Jenna's place. They lived halfway up Hillridge Road, in the mountains north of town, with miles of forest between them and their nearest neighbor. Jenna said her great-grandfather had built the house, and it had been passed on from father to son for three generations. Jenna being an only child, I guessed it would pass to her next, although I couldn't imagine her wanting to live out there in the sticks for the rest of her life.

They had a big gravel yard out front. I pulled up next to her dad's beat-up tractor, got out and peered into the surrounding forest. There'd been no sign of the black pickup on the way up here, but then, on the narrow, winding road there wouldn't be many places to hide something of that size. Unless you used someone's driveway. If, however, someone was on foot, or even on a motorcycle, it would be easy to hide in the woods and not be seen.

Jenna didn't look sick at all when she answered the door, which only increased my suspicion that she was staying home because of the threats. We closeted ourselves in her room and talked about the game. I have to admit to bragging about the triangle offense. Sure, we still might have won, but that was the turning point of the game, and Jenna had been so sure Coach Scott wouldn't use it.

"Those messages stop yet?" I asked casually when there was a lull in the conversation.

"No," said Jenna. She looked up at me as if she knew I wouldn't like what she was about to say. "I messaged him back again."

I pulled away from her as if she'd bitten me. "What? Jenna, of all the stupid—"

"I knew you'd say that." She was defiant.

"I thought we agreed you wouldn't contact him again. You can't get into a conversation with this guy. It'll only make it worse."

The look on her face told me it already was worse. I sat back down on the bed.

"Okay, tell me what happened."

Jenna took a deep breath. "I sent him a message saying I'd keep quiet, that he didn't have to worry about me. If he stopped the messages, I'd never go to the police."

"And?"

"And he said that wasn't good enough. That I still had the evidence and he couldn't trust me. So I asked him again, *What evidence?* and he got really angry. Said, *I'm tired of your games. You know what evidence I mean.* But I don't know!"

She looked confused and scared. I didn't know how much more of this she could take.

I put my arm around her, and she leaned into me. I felt helpless. There had to be something we could do.

"When exactly did these messages start?" I asked her.

She sat up and blew her nose. "I don't know exactly," she said. "Until Noah told me to keep them, I'd delete them right away." She shuddered. I could imagine how it would feel to have them sitting on your phone and your computer. A constant reminder that someone was stalking you.

"Well, approximately then," I said.

She thought for a minute. "A few weeks ago now. Maybe early February?"

"And they came in through Facebook?" An idea was starting to form in my mind.

She nodded.

"Let's see what you posted around that time then," I said, getting up and sitting at her desk in front of the computer. "Maybe he saw something there that started this whole thing."

She nudged me over and squeezed onto the seat with me, and we scrolled through her posts, looking back to February. I couldn't think of anything different or unusual that had happened around that time. School was in. The regular basketball season was coming to a close, with playoffs just around the corner. Jenna's team had been doing well, but they were a good team. It's not like there was any game fixing going on or anything.

We scrolled right back to January and then moved forward again. At first glance, there didn't seem to be anything unusual— photos from basketball games, Amber's birthday, a concert Jenna and I had gone to in Portland a few weeks earlier. There were selfies taken goofing around with her friends at school, photos with her cousin Mel from Canada, pictures of her two dogs, quotes she'd taken off the Internet, a pencil drawing Amber had done for her in art class. It was the usual stuff.

"Wasn't your cousin here back in December?" I asked. It was the only thing that seemed out of place.

"Yeah, she left right after New Year's," said Jenna. "I didn't get around to posting the pictures of her visit for a while though."

I flicked back to those pictures and looked more closely at the date. She'd posted them on February 3. Right around the time she started getting the messages. But a month after Mel went back to Victoria.

"When did she leave exactly?" I said.

"January 2," said Jenna. "This picture here was taken the day she left. We stopped at the 7-Eleven on the way to..." Her voice trailed off. I didn't need her to finish the sentence. That was the day the 7-Eleven had been robbed. And she'd been a witness who had seen nothing. Or had she?

I clicked on the photo, and Jenna's and Mel's faces filled the screen. They were standing with their backs to the store, grinning at the camera. They'd always been great friends as well as cousins. In the larger version of the photo, we both now saw what hadn't been so clear before. There was a male figure opening the door to the 7-Eleven behind them. Dressed in a gray hoodie and jeans, he fit the description from Crime Stoppers. I zoomed in. The man was looking over his shoulder, as if scouting the area, and his face was clearly visible.

"Oh my god," said Jenna.

"*Oh-my-god*," I repeated with emphasis.

It was Jesse Derby.

Chapter Twelve

Jesse Derby. I couldn't believe it. He was a teammate. A low-life, betraying sneak of a teammate, but still a teammate. The idea of him having participated in the robbery of the 7-Eleven was unthinkable. And yet the evidence was right in front of me.

"This is it," I said. "This is why you're getting those messages from Nick Smith. He's probably the other guy you saw who they've been talking about on Crime Stoppers—the one with the leather jacket."

"But Jesse Derby?" said Jenna. "What's he doing mixed up in something like this?"

"I don't know. He's always kept pretty much to himself. Especially these last couple of months." And no wonder, I thought. He was freaking out, worrying that Jenna would take this photo to the police.

"You know you have to go to the cops with this," I said.

She stood up and started pacing. "Dylan, that's exactly what I can't do," she said. "These guys mean business."

"Which is why you have to go to the cops." I took her hands, forcing her to stop walking. "Jenna, you can't let them get away with it. With the robbery or the stalking."

She looked down at our hands, fingers entwined, and said nothing. I couldn't tell what she was thinking. And I could only imagine what she was feeling.

"If you bury this, they've won," I said. "And you'll never have any peace of mind. You'll always be looking over your shoulder, wondering if they're still watching you."

Still nothing.

"Jenna...?"

Finally, she looked up at me. "Okay," she said. "You're right. I mean, how could I go to school and face Jesse Derby knowing what I know now? But Dyl...I'm scared."

"I know," I said, pulling her close. I was scared too.

We set off for town in my Civic. Neither of us said much. The air in the car was practically crackling with tension. The whole situation seemed surreal, like something out of a movie. This wasn't Jenna and me racing into town with evidence of a crime, it was some other teenage couple. Some kids out of a movie driving down a dark, lonely road. In a minute it would start to rain or snow, and they would smash into a fallen tree or skid off into the ravine, never to be seen again.

I slowed down a bit and tightened my grip on the steering wheel. The last thing I wanted was to have an accident on the way to town. There was no hurry. It wasn't like the cop shop closed at six o'clock or anything.

They would be there whenever we arrived, and we would show them the photo and tell them what had been happening to Jenna. That had to be enough to arrest Jesse Derby, and Nick Smith as well—or, at least, enough to bring Nick in for questioning.

Lights appeared in my rearview mirror. Great. That was all I needed. Some local tailing me down the road, impatient for his night out or something.

Suddenly, the lights came toward us. They loomed up as if we were at a standstill. I felt a thump from behind, and my heart rate went from 75 to 175 in less than a second.

"Dylan, it's the black pickup!" cried Jenna. There was real fear in her voice. She knew as well as I did that this was no coincidence. "It's them," she said. "Hurry, Dylan, it's them!"

I didn't need any urging. I sped down the mountain as fast as I dared. I careened around corners, tires squealing, and raced through the straight stretches. I could only hope that if there was a car coming up the hill, I would see its headlights before I smashed into it head-on.

"I can't shake them," I said.

Jenna was frantically punching 9-1-1 into her phone.

"Someone's trying to run us off the road," she said into the phone. "We're on—"

I whipped around another corner, and she lost the signal.

"Damn," she said, trying desperately to get them back.

The pickup slammed into us again. Jenna screamed.

I didn't want to slow down. I knew what had happened last time when I'd done that. But we were approaching Devil's Bend, and there was no way I could take it at the speed we were going.

"Hold on," I said. I went into the bend and hit the brakes. With tires screeching, we skidded around the corner, inches away from the metal barrier. I managed to stop us from going into a spin, but we'd lost a lot of speed. As we came onto the straight, the pickup pulled out alongside us.

It swerved toward us, just like it had the time before. I held my ground. There wasn't much room to maneuver. I couldn't let him force me off the road again. The truck bumped the side of the Civic, and my side mirror crumpled.

"Do something, Dylan," said Jenna.

"Like what?"

We rounded the next bend side by side, so close that if I'd opened my window I could have touched the side of the truck. If we met anyone coming the other way, we were doomed. I sped up out of the corner, hoping to get ahead of him, but he kept pace. He drifted closer, and I felt the crunch of gravel under my tires. I twisted my steering wheel to the left, and the car slammed against the pickup. My little Honda was a featherweight fighting against a heavyweight though. It was no contest. The truck didn't budge.

I was tempted to stop. Get out of the car and haul Nick Smith out of the truck, demand to know what he was doing. But there was no guarantee he would let me get near the truck. Truck versus Civic was bad enough. Truck versus man was a disaster. Besides, even if he did get out of the truck, I doubted he was the talking kind. He'd proven that he would go to any length to get what he wanted. And we couldn't delete that photo. We couldn't let him get away with this, or Jenna would never be truly free of him.

I was close to losing control though. Somehow we had to get away from him.

We came to a straight section of road, and I hit the gas.

"Hang on—I'm gonna try something," I said.

When I was almost at the corner, I stomped on the brake. The tires screamed, and the truck shot past us. I slammed the car into Reverse and hit the gas again as the truck skidded to a stop. When I'd gained some distance, I put the car back into Drive. The truck's back-up lights came on. In the next instant, it was barreling toward us. I stomped my foot down.

"Dylan, are you crazy?" yelled Jenna.

"I hope not," I said through gritted teeth.

I wrenched the wheel hard to the left. The car veered around the truck, and we took the corner at top speed. I knew there was a driveway on the other side. The Marshalls'. If I could reach it before the truck got going again, we might have a chance.

We fishtailed out of the turn, and I saw the Marshalls' mailbox up ahead. I stepped on the gas and swung into the driveway without slowing down. Switching off the Honda's lights, I eased up on the gas. I couldn't afford to put the brakes on. Any light would give away our position. So we bumped along the long dirt driveway toward the Marshalls' house in the dark, hoping beyond hope that Nick Smith hadn't seen us turn off.

I saw the headlights of the truck go past and glanced over at Jenna. We were safe. For now. It wouldn't be long before he realized we weren't ahead of him, though, and what would he do then?

Chapter Thirteen

The Marshalls weren't home. I parked the Civic behind some trees and turned off the engine. If anyone came into the yard, they would see us, but we were hidden from the road. It was the best I could do.

"9-1-1. What is your emergency?" I heard faintly from Jenna's phone. She'd gotten a signal.

"Someone just chased us down Hillridge Road," Jenna said in a surprisingly calm voice.

She's always been good in emergencies. I couldn't stop my hands from shaking. I peered into the trees, searching for lights. "They tried to run us off the road, rammed us with their truck."

The voice on the phone said something I couldn't hear, and Jenna answered.

"We turned into a driveway, but we're scared he'll come back."

Another question.

"Yeah, I got the license-plate number. It's..."

I grabbed Jenna's arm. "Jenna. There are headlights on the road." If he came up the driveway, we were sitting ducks. "We've got to get out of here."

Jenna looked at her cell and swore loudly. "My phone just died."

We jumped out of the car and dashed into the woods surrounding the Marshalls' house. A short distance away, we stopped, crouched behind a large bush and peered back at the Marshalls' yard. I could hear Jenna panting and knew her heart must be racing as fast as mine. I took her hand and gave it a squeeze. Whatever happened, we were in it together.

The lights turned into the driveway. For a brief instant I fooled myself into thinking it might be the Marshalls coming home, but that hope was quickly dashed as the Ford F-150 pulled into the yard. It stopped in front of the house, and someone got out of the driver's side. As he walked through the beam of the headlights toward my car, I saw that it wasn't Nick Smith at all. It was Jesse Derby.

Jenna and I looked at each other in surprise. I guess we both had been thinking that Nick Smith was the mastermind of this whole thing. That Jesse had been coerced into giving him information about Jenna, had somehow been an unwilling participant in betraying his teammates. This was clearly not the case.

In unspoken agreement, we both started backing away.

Jesse slammed his hand on the hood of my car, kicked the front tire and let forth a stream of swearing. Then he turned his gaze to the woods.

We didn't wait to see any more. We ran.

We should have tried to be quieter, but panic does things to your brain. It goes into fight-or-flight mode, and our brains were telling us to fly.

In the darkness of the forest, we tripped and stumbled on roots, crashed through bushes, ran into unseen branches. In short, we must have sounded like a couple of Sasquatches running through the woods.

I could hear Jesse crashing through the trees behind us. We had a head start, but only just. I glanced back to see exactly how close he was. Big mistake. I couldn't see past the nearest tree anyway and ended up flat on my face, tripping over a rock.

Jenna dragged me up.

"Come on," she whispered, like we hadn't been making any noise at all. "This way."

I didn't know where we were going, only that we were running downhill and at the bottom of the hill was town. But Jenna had grown up on this mountain. She'd spent her whole life walking and running on its trails. I didn't think much of it was secret to her.

I followed her up a small rise and onto something that resembled a track. The going was a bit easier here, and a bit of moonlight filtered through the gaps in the trees. We raced along, leaping over roots and fallen branches. I thought Jenna must have cat eyes. She saw obstacles on the path long before I did and pulled me out of their way before I could trip on them.

At last, we slowed near a stream running alongside the path. Jenna put her finger to her lips to warn me to be quiet. I urged her to hurry. I could hear Jesse approaching in the distance. Jenna crept down the bank to the water's edge, then stepped out onto a rock and jumped across to the other side. I followed.

It seemed like a dead end. The bank on this side of the stream rose to a rock face that would be difficult to climb. I had to trust that Jenna knew what she was doing.

We crept quietly upstream for a few yards and stopped near a bush. Jenna pulled some branches aside and disappeared behind them. I slipped in after her.

It was as dark as the inside of a box in there. As my eyes adjusted, I realized we were in a small cave, no more than a few feet deep. There was a sliver of light filtering through the bush at the entrance. From outside, you couldn't tell the cave was even there.

I held my breath as I heard Jesse nearing our hiding spot. He wasn't making any attempt to be quiet. He was wheezing like crazy and muttering under his breath. He'd slowed down, obviously realizing he couldn't hear us anymore. His footsteps stopped almost directly across from the cave, and I could imagine him looking around, listening, trying to figure out which way we had gone. I didn't dare peek out.

In the darkness of the cave, I couldn't see Jenna beside me, but I could feel that she was holding her breath as well. Our hands were locked together, my fingers aching under her grip. She was trembling.

Jesse went a little farther along the track. I could hear him swearing and cursing. It sounded like he was searching the bushes near the track, smashing each one with a large stick, maybe a baseball bat. Or was it a rifle? My imagination was running wild. With each crash, Jenna jumped a little. I let go of her hands and pulled her closer.

She wasn't expecting it, and her foot scraped along the floor of the cave as she tried to keep her balance. It sounded like a firecracker to us. I closed my eyes, cursing myself for my stupidity.

We waited, expecting at any second to hear Jesse crossing the stream. Expecting the bush to be wrenched away from the entrance to the cave, our hiding place revealed.

It didn't happen.

The smashing of bushes slowed and then stopped. There was silence for what seemed like an eternity. And then a scream of rage and frustration. Jesse's footsteps moved back along the track the way he had come and faded into silence.

We waited a full five minutes before we dared to ease the bush aside and peer out of our hiding spot. There was no sign of Jesse, and the only sounds were the normal night rustles of the forest. Cautiously, we crept out, recrossed the stream and climbed back up to the track.

We couldn't risk going back to the Marshalls'. For all we knew, Jesse was there waiting for us. So we picked our way down the mountain toward town. Silently at first, fearful that Jesse was still lurking somewhere, waiting for us to reveal ourselves. But as time moved on and nothing happened, we relaxed and made better progress.

It wasn't an easy hike—at least a couple of miles of dense forest. We stuck to the track when we could, but at times Jenna deviated from it, cutting through the woods and, miraculously, finding another track on the other side. If it hadn't been for her, I would have been hopelessly lost.

By the time we got close to town, fear had turned into exhaustion. I called

Noah and asked him to pick us up on the highway. It felt good to be back in civilization, sitting in Noah's Frontier, the heater on and a good solid vehicle around us. Safe, although I couldn't help glancing behind us once in a while to make sure we weren't being followed.

We filled Noah in on everything that had happened on the way to the police station. He wasn't as shocked as we were about Jesse Derby.

"I never liked that guy," he said. "Not since kindergarten, when he stole chips and candy bars out of everyone's lunchboxes." He laughed in a rueful way. "Not that anyone caught him doing it, but I was pretty sure it was him."

I guess Jesse had a longer history of thieving than I'd thought.

It was after ten by the time we arrived at the police station. Jenna and I must have looked like we'd been in a gang war. Our faces were scratched, our clothes torn. Jenna had huge dark circles under her eyes. I was nervous and relieved at the same time as we finally walked through the glass doors and into the station. As luck would have it, the officer who had interviewed Jenna about the robbery was on duty when we arrived.

"What happened to you?" he said, looking from Jenna to me and back again.

"Can we sit down?" said Jenna. "It's a long story."

Chapter Fourteen

We didn't see Jesse Derby at school again after that.

An hour after walking into the police station, Officer Keene sent someone out to bring both Jesse Derby and Nick Smith in for questioning. There was plenty of evidence. We had the photo of Jesse outside the 7-Eleven on the day and at the exact time of the robbery. We had the photo of the black pickup with damage to its rear bumper. We even had evidence to support our claim that Jesse had tried to run us off the road that night. The Marshalls had called in earlier to report two damaged vehicles in their yard, a silver Honda Civic and a black Ford F-150. Needless to say, the license-plate number of the pickup matched the one in the photo I'd taken in Vancouver. That, along with all the threatening messages Jenna had received, would make a convincing case against Jesse and Nick.

Word got around school that Jesse had been charged in the 7-Eleven robbery, and rumors were flying about why he had done it. Some people said he'd gotten mixed up with a gang. Others said the whole family was a bunch of thugs and thieves, and he was following the family business. A few even claimed that his dad was dying of cancer, and Jesse needed money to pay the hospital bills. Only Jesse knew the real truth. I did find out two things for sure—one, that Nick Smith was Jesse's brother-in-law, who had moved here a year ago after some trouble in Detroit, and two, Jesse had been in trouble with the law before, and now that he was eighteen, he'd be tried in adult court. Which may have scared him enough to try to stop Jenna from giving her photo to the police. I didn't envy him a prison sentence if he was convicted.

Coach Scott wasn't happy about losing someone from the team, not with the regional semis only a few days away. It would be tough going with only one sub. Luckily, Stretch got the go-ahead from his doctor to start playing again. Not a full green light, but an amber, which meant I kept my spot on the starting five, and we had two more tall players in reserve. Not a bad outcome all around.

The weekend flew past faster than a fighter jet, and suddenly it was game day. With everything that had been happening, my mind hadn't really been on basketball. I'd even missed a practice because Officer Keene stopped in at the school to ask Jenna and me a few more questions. But as the bus chugged down the road toward Vancouver, headed for Hudson's Bay High, all I could think about was playoffs. We were in the regional semis, two steps away from the State Championship. My nerves were jumping.

Piling off the bus in front of the school, we made a lot of noise and tried to swagger in like this was just another game, that we'd been to playoffs tons of times before. I don't think anyone was fooled. We were all nervous, and you could see it, even during the warm-up. We'd never played Hudson's Bay before, and though Coach had assured us they were beatable, it was the unknown that was unnerving us.

Our squad of supporters and cheerleaders was a drop in the ocean of Hudson's Bay fans. Hudson's Bay was a big school, and it looked like the whole student body had turned out to cheer them on. I gave Jenna a nervous smile as we ran on for the jump ball and saw her yell, "Go, Dylan!" but her voice was lost in the crowd. All I could hear was "Eagles! Eagles! Eagles!" Then the whistle blew for the start of the game.

It started off badly. I missed the tip-off, and Hudson's Bay scored in the first ten seconds. From there it went downhill, if that's even possible. Yeah, we made a few baskets, got a few rebounds and stole the ball off them a couple of times, but compared to the fouls and missed shots and bad passes, it wasn't nearly enough. The fact is, we pretty much stunk in the first half.

Coach Scott was tearing his hair out, and we didn't get the usual "you can do it" speech at halftime. We all sat around, glum and discouraged, waiting for him to say something, to pump us up and get us going again. We got nothing. He paced the floor of the locker room, shaking his head for so long I thought maybe he'd just given up on us.

Finally, he looked up and said, "Chelseas. Think of them as Chelseas. No better, no worse. Now go out there and stop playing like a bunch of freshmen."

We looked at each other and laughed nervously.

"Go on. Move it!" he said.

We jumped up. We all knew what he meant. And he was right. We were letting the pressure of playoffs get to us. This was just another game, and if we didn't treat it like that, we were going to lose for sure.

As I headed for the door, Coach pulled me aside. "One day you're going to have to explain that to me, Lane."

I grinned and ran after the team.

Coach's words seemed to have sunk in with everyone. Suddenly, we were a team again, anticipating moves, reading the ball handler, following through on the plays that Coach called. Isaiah was on fire in the paint, and Matt's three-pointers were hitting the mark as well. Even Noah seemed to come alive. Slowly, the score started creeping up.

And then, with seven minutes left on the clock, the most amazing thing happened. I was playing point guard, and Noah was center. I brought the ball down the court, passed it to Matt and headed for the outside corner. The Eagles defense wasn't letting anyone into the key, and we passed the ball around the perimeter, looking for an opening. I'd just taken a pass from Spence when Isaiah ducked into an open spot in the lane. I fired it in to him, and he drove in for the layup. Hudson's Bay was having none of that, though, and Isaiah pulled up and shot the ball back out to Matt. Matt went for the outside shot, but it bounced off the rim. Noah grabbed the rebound and, with only two seconds left on the shot clock, popped it back up for a second try at the basket.

It went in.

"Yeah!" I yelled, jumping up and down.

Noah's grin took over his whole face. I thumped him on the back as we ran to take our positions at the other end of the court, and all the guys high-fived him. Even Coach was smiling.

That was the high point of the game. Despite our effort, it wasn't enough. We'd fallen so far behind in the first half, we would have had to stop Hudson's Bay from scoring completely to win. And that was impossible. They were good. There was no denying that. If we'd gotten our act together from the first whistle, it would have been a contest. As it was, we lost by fifteen points.

You would have thought the mood on the bus going back to school would have been pretty somber. We'd lost, after all. But we knew we'd played damn good basketball in the second half, and a score of 75-90 was nothing to be ashamed of. We'd put Mountview High on the basketball scoreboard for the first time in ten years.

Jenna and I were pretty quiet amid the chatter and back slapping and rehashing of game plays going on around us. The tension of the last few weeks was catching up with me, and it must have been even worse for her.

Carlos weaved his way down the aisle and thumped into the seat in front of us, next to Noah.

"So, you win," he said to Jenna. "I guess it's my round of sodas after all." He punched Noah in the shoulder. "I really didn't think you had it in you."

Jenna gave Carlos a furious look. We'd never told Noah about the bet. We didn't think he'd ever have agreed to train with us if he knew, and now that we'd gotten to know him...well, it all seemed rather callous.

"What do you mean?" said Jenna, flustered. "Why would you want to buy us a round of sodas?"

"Don't worry," said Noah. "I know about the bet."

Jenna's face went red. I hadn't seen that happen very often.

"And you're not mad?" she said.

"Why would I be mad?" he said. "This is the first time in four years I've actually felt like part of the team. No more Noah Stumblefoot."

We laughed awkwardly. We'd all been guilty of calling him that, if not to his face, then behind his back.

Jenna turned to Carlos. "But the bet was for last week's game. I lost."

Carlos elbowed Noah in the ribs. "The big man here went double or nothing. It's sodas for the girls' team too." He high-fived Noah. "Nice shot."

A ball of paper hit Carlos in the back of the head, and he jumped up to fire it back.

"Double or nothing?" Jenna said to Noah.

Noah shrugged. "Why not? I had nothing to lose," he said and turned to face the front of the bus again.

I found out later that Noah had been at the rec center practicing his shooting all weekend. You had to hand it to the guy— when he put his mind to something, he didn't do it halfway.

Jenna's phone vibrated in her pocket, and she pulled it out to check the message.

"Everything okay?" I said when her expression didn't change. "It's not another message from Nick Smith, is it?" The messages had stopped after we went to the police, but we were a bit nervous now that Jesse Derby and Nick Smith were out on bail.

"No," she said. "It's an email from Officer Keene. The court date has been set."

She put the phone back in her pocket and stared out the window, and I slid my hand over hers. It was over, but it wasn't.

As the key witness, Jenna had a lot to do before she'd be allowed to forget about the last couple of months. If she ever could.

The ball of paper flew over us, then suddenly whizzed past my ear and hit Jenna on the side of the head.

With mock indignation, she snatched it off the seat and fired it up the bus. It hit Coach Scott in the back. Jenna looked at me, then swore softly and ducked down in her seat, giggling.

"Lane?" said Coach, holding up the ball of paper. "Did this come from you?"

"No, sir," I said, trying to keep a straight face.

He glared at everyone, then turned back toward the front of the bus.

I slunk down next to Jenna. "No, sir," she mimicked silently, and we burst into laughter. We kept our heads down as we watched Noah tear a sheet of paper out of his notebook, crumple it into a ball and send it out over our heads.

Things were changing, there was no denying it. It suddenly hit me that this was our last bus ride back to school as a team. This time next year, with Stretch at UCLA, Noah out on the east coast somewhere and Carlos at flight school, we'd be spread across the country. I didn't even know if Jenna and I would still be together. She was smart. She'd probably have her pick of colleges.

I gave her hand a squeeze and she smiled at me, a smile that turned into a laugh as my stomach growled louder than a German shepherd in attack mode.

I laughed with her. One thing I did know—the whole team was probably famished. And there was a booth at Jo's Diner with our name on it.

Acknowledgments

I am indebted to my husband, Russell, for his help while I was writing this novel, not only for his support, which is unending, but for reading the manuscript and providing suggestions on the technicalities of basketball. Research can only go so far, and without his expertise this book would not have come to a happy conclusion. Thanks also to my editor, Amy Collins, for fielding my many questions regarding basketball in North American high schools, as my experience with the sport has been in Australian schools only. Lastly, I would also like to acknowledge my daughters, whose involvement in basketball gave me the idea for the story, with special thanks to Claudia for reading the manuscript and providing a teen perspective.

Sonya Spreen Bates is a Canadian writer living in South Australia. She writes for children and adults, and her stories have been published in Australia, New Zealand and Canada. *Off the Rim* is her second book in the Orca Sports series.

orca sports

For more information on all the books
in the Orca Sports series, please visit
www.orcabook.com.